The Dead Club

A Frank DeGrae Case

Christopher Allen

ISBN: 9798642906965
Imprint: Independently Published
May 18, 2020
by Cris A. Cannon
Send inquiries to: 110 Hill Street
Wilsonville, Alabama 35186
book2017@yahoo.com

Janet von Gal, Editor
Sine Die

Dedication

This book is dedicated to the memory of my late wife, Linda. She was instrumental in supporting my early efforts of writing. This book was started while she was still here. It remained unfinished for a very long time when she became ill and afterwards. It is with great pleasure I am able to publish the finished project on and for Linda's birthday, May 18th.
Happy Birthday Linda. You are greatly missed.

'Chris Allen'

This novel's story and characters are fictitious and any similarities to real persons, living or deceased, are purely coincidental. Although certain long standing institutions, businesses, agencies, and public offices may be mentioned, the characters involved and story are wholly imaginary.

1

It was 2:05 o'clock, ante meridiem, when the phone rang. Gradually the ringing grew louder until the bell sounded like a fire alarm. I stirred from the best sleep I'd had in ages and was a bit disoriented at first. Still discombobulated and quite irritated I managed to grab the receiver even in the dark.

"What!?" I shouted as I was still trying to wake up.

"Frank?" crackled a voice from across the wire.

"What? Who is this?" I shouted while trying to rise and fumble with the lamp. At the same time I caught it from falling off the bedside table.

"Frank, I'm on another one. We just got the call a little while ago and I've been here only a few minutes but it's the same as the last one."

I was somewhat awake now beginning to sit up on the side of the bed. Leaning forward and slightly off balance I managed to turn the lamp on as my feet hit the floor. "Where are you?"

"55 Central Park West. One of the guys in the lobby'll bring you up when you get here."

Still groggy I reached over and turned the Big Ben where I could see it better. I replied, "Alright Cal, I'll be right over."

Hanging the receiver back on the candlestick I know I mumbled something but even I didn't know what it was. Still trying to clear my head I picked the clock up from the night stand and started winding the key. I don't think it really needed it but I turned the key about three times before setting it back on the table. I was just wasting time trying to work up to standing. It was almost 2:30 when I shook a Camel from its pack and jammed it in my lips. Tossing the crumpled, nearly empty pack back on the night table I picked up the Zippo as I stood.

By the light of the dim bedside lamp I walked toward the bathroom. Reaching the doorway across the small high-ceilinged room I lit the fag and set the lighter on the dresser. As I took that first long drag I continued in. I thought it would help wake me up a bit but all it did was make me cough. Pushing the wall switch button inside next to the door the single bulb over the sink flickered to life. I sat the cigarette on the edge of the counter with the hot end hanging over the edge and found myself looking back at me from the mirror. I grumbled something unintelligible again and took another draw from the smoke. I looked rough and felt worse.

I finally realized I needed to pick up the pace a little and tossed the butt into the john. At the brief hiss of the hot ember I reached past my straight razor and picked up the three-piece Gillette. I knew I could get through that ritual much faster with it. Since it was already apart I was going to put in a fresh blade until I noticed the box was empty. Note to self; pick up a box of Blue Blades. I had to fall back to the straight razor for now.

In recent months Lieutenant Akers had been assigned to work a few murders that started to look connected. There seemed to be a number of similarities but the dots hadn't quite been connected just yet. It appeared he found another one tonight. I would find out soon enough.

oOo

From my place on East 57th Street I drove up Lexington Avenue to 65th Street. A left onto 65th took me through Central Park and I was there in just a few minutes. The street in front of the building was jammed with official vehicles so I circled the block looking for a place to park. I finally parked where I first arrived, around the corner from the apartment building at the church next door.

When I walked into the lobby there were surprisingly few people standing around. Mostly newshounds and scribblers. Whoever was upstairs must be worthy of a spot in the papers.

"Mr. DeGrae?" came a voice from behind me. As I turned to see who was calling I heard again, "Mr. DeGrae, I'm to escort you upstairs sir."

A fresh-faced young lady in uniform came into view as I pivoted around. "Lieutenant Akers assigned me to stand by down here and take you up to the scene, sir."

"Very well young lady", I answered.

"Officer", she said.

"Excuse me?" I responded.

With the same monotone professional tone she replied with, "Officer. Officer Brant. Cynthia Brant, sir. Shall we?" as she turned while gesturing and started across the lobby toward the elevators. I started to ask a question but found myself following trying to catch up.

Once on the elevator the operator closed the door and pulled the inner mesh gate while turning the lever to ascend. It was obvious he already knew where we were going since no one spoke to him. I asked Officer Brant, "So how long have you been with the department?" My question was further punctuated with a slight jolt and metallic clanging sound as the elevator began its ascent.

"Well sir, I just completed my training last year."

"Last year? I see."

After a short pause and another clang and lurch of the elevator Brant continued with, "Yes sir. I was in the first group to take the new Policewoman civil service exam in '38."

"I see." This was followed by another somewhat awkward pause as the elevator continued its ascent accompanied by a monotone humming sound of the drive gear. Before either of us could speak again the silence was broken by the operator slowing the car and gradually coming to an unusually smooth stop.

As the door slid into the wall and the attendant pulled open the inner gate Officer Brant stated, "Sir, if you will turn left as you exit the elevator you will find Lieutenant Akers down in apartment 1010."

As I stepped off the elevator I uttered, "Thank you officer". I commenced my stroll down the long narrow causeway. Ornately carpeted and lined with intermittent accent lighting that gave a Victorian era appearance, I could see a group of people huddled near a door at the turn of the hall where the other wing met this one. It wasn't long before I realized Brant had followed me off the elevator and was walking behind me. I was only now beginning to get the impression of how important this case was going to be. It appeared that Calvin intended for me to show up regardless of what was going on otherwise.

The apartment wasn't hard to find. The door was open and the hall was filled with New York's finest. Some were in uniform but most were not. As I approached all heads turned and looked in our direction. "Hello boys. Lieutenant Akers around?" I asked.

"Come on in Frank", came a voice from the group. At first an arm appeared. Then the rest of the attached person emerged from the perimeter of the huddle to greet me. "Akers is inside waiting for you. Come on", he said as he simultaneously spun back around and headed back into the pack. I followed.

"So what's up Carl?" I asked as we pushed our way into the apartment. Or should I say as Carl pushed through. I kept directly behind him letting him do the work.

"Make a hole! Move it fellas!" exclaimed Sergeant Williams to his men before acknowledging me. "It looks like some of you guys need to go back to the lobby or back on the street. You, Jimmy, you handle it. Clear this hallway."

"Yes Sergeant" answered someone in the crowd. Carl and I continued as we were and turned into the apartment entrance.

Carl continued, "I'll just let the lieutenant run it down to you since he's right around the corner".

Before I could say anything to Carl we turned that corner and there stood Akers. As we entered he turned to look in our direction. The front parlor area appeared to be nothing more than an extension of the hallway's Victorian look. A very large and spacious room with a transom window over every door. There were even tandem transom windows situated side-by-side above the large twin pocket doors leading to a large formal dining room. The original high narrowly slatted ceiling complete with a large slowly rotating ceiling fan was still in place and the interior wall fire place had been enclosed but otherwise still intact. However, someone had installed a rather large Allen's parlor furnace against the north-facing exterior wall. It probably dated from the 20s, or earlier, and hadn't be used in a while either. Heat to the apartment was now furnished as was the rest of the building by radiators.

I was glad to see Akers' humor hadn't been damaged yet. His facial expression morphed from a somber scowl to raised eyebrows complete with a large vaudevillian, Joe E. Brown, ear to ear grin. "Frank!" he said as he reached out in my direction to grab my hand. "It's really good to see you. Come here. I've got another one in there." Pointing into a nearby bedroom and shaking my hand he turned back away from me while saying, "Come here Frank. You've got to see this."

"Well, hello Calvin. It's good seeing you too", I answered while looking at the back of his head.

As we entered the room I took no more than two or three steps and stopped cold in my tracks. "Oh, I see what you mean. It is another one. So Calvin, how many does this make now?"

"This one is number five Frank. Five in as many months."

Just as I was about to inquire further came the impromptu, "Well hello gentlemen. So what do we have here?" from the hall.

Looking toward the door I replied, "Well, good morning counsellor. You're out awfully early."

"Funny Frank. Why are you here?"

Calvin spoke up saying, "He's here because I called for him Miss McKinley."

"Thank you lieutenant." Marion turned back to me and asked again, "So, Frank, why are you in my crime scene?"

"Well Marion, I guess I could ask the same of you. I know you're working in the DA's office now but how did you find out about this thing so soon? It's 3:00 A.M. on a Sunday morning and you look nice. I mean you don't look like you just got up. I mean—"

"Enough Frank. Stop", she finished for me. "You know the Manhattan District Attorney's Office has a call taker on weekends and I'm the on-call Assistant DA this weekend. And, if it's any of your business, I was out with someone tonight."

"Well, no, it's not any of my business. Not anymore. But thanks for the disclosure. So how is Mr. Dewey?"

At hearing the District Attorney's name Marion became incensed. I thought she would blow a gasket. Her face was contorted with indignation as she barked, "That's quite enough Frank. That's not even remotely funny. I suggest you reel in the sarcasm or I will have you removed from here right now."

"Alright, alright Marion. I guess that was a little over the top. I apologize. I'll stop. Friends again?"

"No. Not friends but I'll leave you and Lieutenant Akers to your work. Lieutenant."

"Yes ma'am."

"Just give me a quick rundown and I'll be on my way."

"Yes ma'am." Calvin turned and made his exit with Marion in tow. I was actually glad our sparring was over and felt sorry for Cal having to still put up with her.

Having returned to the front parlor I began to aimlessly amble about. The building was only about ten years old but some of the architectural features looked to be much older. A very classic style of construction. The transom windows were even highly ornate and oversized for great ventilation. After my first lap around the room I even noticed a pair of huge, ornately carved, oak pocket doors in the walls. My curiosity got the best of me and I pulled them slightly from their nesting places to inspect them closer. It was almost a shame these doors remained out of sight all the time.

After a short while I started checking out the smaller, more mundane, features of my surroundings. I walked over near the window and scanned over the top of a small writing desk. The other window on the other wall had been modified to accommodate the Allen furnace's venting. Looking beyond the desk and out the window revealed an idyllic view of Central Park. There was a hint of sunrise now and the park and streets were beginning to emerge from the darkness.

Momentarily lost in my world Cal and Marion entered the room still engaged in conversation. I turned from the window to face them as they walked in.

"Well Marion, I trust you've seen what you needed to."

Stopping only to pierce me with her contempt filled eyes came, "Frank, there's only one reason you're here and talking to me." With that she made an abrupt turn and walked to the other end of the sofa. Without stopping she scooped up a small clutch purse from the end table and continued to the door.

At the sound of her leaving the apartment Cal chimed in with, "Wow Frank, what's the deal with her?"

"As if you didn't know."

"Well, I guess maybe I do. Sorta'. Never mind. I don't want to know any more than what I saw."

"Probably for the best. So, do I get the nickel tour back there too?"

"Come on", he replied while spinning back around and gesturing with his hand. I was right behind him.

As we turned out of the hallway and back into what appeared to be the master bedroom suite I made an abrupt stop. Lieutenant Akers continued on toward the bed and I scanned around the room taking in the overall picture before proceeding. Once inside there was little question it was the master bedroom suite. The room was massive for a bedroom. It must have been at least thirty-five feet long and nearly that across. Entering the room one immediately stepped onto rich burgundy wall-to-wall carpeting laced with delicate Kelly green vine and leaf designs. To the left was a custom walk-in combination closet and dressing room complete with the cabinets and settee needed to properly take full advantage of such a setup. It appeared the smaller room had been erected more recently than anything else present. The carpeting looked as if it were the same piece of textile as what ran throughout the rest of the bedroom. Not matched. The same piece. The closet walls had been framed up on top of the existing carpet. Even so, the construction had been contracted with a professional. It had been finished and blended in flawlessly.

Looking back toward the rest of the bedroom from the closet door the crime scene came back into view. There was the typical high ceiling with ceiling fan and lighting. Closer examination of the overhead fixture was another hint the walk-in closet had been a relatively new addition. It was off center in relation to the existing bedroom space.

"Frank, look here. See what I mean?"

I walked on over to Calvin and he was right. Lying face down in the middle of a large full-size heavy gauge brass framed bed was a gentleman of about thirty-five years of age wearing nothing but an Italian Sferra Giza cotton bedsheet worth more than my car and a large pair of pinking shears sunk into the middle of his back between the shoulder blades. "Well, I guess you're right Cal. It sure looks like the others."

"It sure does", he said. "What do you make of this Frank? Maybe a call girl exacting her revenge? If this isn't the work of the same person it sure is lookin' like it."

"I agree. These scenes all look entirely too staged. I don't mean the crime scene or evidence has been staged or tampered with. I mean the killer sets up the prey to be killed this way. I do think this has been the work of a single person and carefully planned out. But I guess the real question is who and why."

Lieutenant Akers continued with, "That reminds me. I've also noticed in the lab reports on the other guys; whoever's doing this is either really lucky or they seem to know how to cover their tracks."

"Oh?"

"Yeah. We haven't been able to find any real evidence. No other blood besides the victim. No prints. No trace evidence on the beds. Nothing."

"Look Cal, I'm going to need to see your case files on the others. When we leave here let's stop somewhere and grab some breakfast."

"Okay, sounds good to me."

"Then we'll head down to your office and I can make some notes", I said.

"Sounds alright to me. I guess if you're getting pulled into this thing like this you need all the information we have."

"Uh...Lieutenant?" was heard from behind us at the door. "Are you ready for us yet?"

Calvin and I walked back to the bedroom door and into the hall not speaking any further. There was just a hint of somber reverence hanging in the air as we met the Medical Examiner guys in the hall with their gurney. With nearly inaudible murmurs we exchanged salutations as we passed. They wrestled the gurney into the bedroom doorway as we made our way to the front door.

"Well there goes another one to 'The Pit'", Calvin said.

"Yeah, I guess so. Ready for breakfast yet?"

"Right behind ya' Frank."

2

The Lieutenant and I took a quick trip down Central Park West to a little place on the other side of Columbus Circle. It was still early and there weren't many places to choose from being a Sunday morning. When I spotted Herrin & Hardy's was open I yelled out to stop. Besides I was kinda' in a hurry to get my hands on Akers' files as much as I wanted a cup of Joe.

"So, you've been awfully quiet. What's on your mind?" asked Akers as he grabbed the fat brass bar of the front door. Pulling the door open I walked past and answered, "I'm not really sure just yet" as I entered. He followed. "I can tell you one thing for sure though Calvin."

"What's that?"

"I need coffee. Where's the urn in this place? Oh, never mind, I see it", I said as I left Calvin standing there looking like a lost puppy. I had to walk past all of the chrome and glass automat doors to the rear of the dining room to finally reach the coffee. I wasn't too concerned about Cal. He'd find his way.

After we finally got our coffees and bagels we found a table in the nearly empty place. "So, Cal, tell me again about the first one."

"Well, it was right around Thanksgiving last year. I remember having to talk to the family just before the holiday. The victim was at his home on 5th Avenue near 37th Street. He was about 40 years old and lived alone. He was a plumber by trade. Nothing remarkable about his life or history. He was found just like this guy was. Stabbed in the back while in bed."

"With those huge scissors?"

"Oh yeah. The same thing."

"Any criminal history?"

"Nothing to speak of really."

"What do you mean by, really?"

"I remember he did show an arrest for assaulting his wife about a year before but he was acquitted."

"That's it? Nothing else?"

"No. That's why I remember it."

"Okay. Let's skip ahead a bit. I can safely assume the rest of the victims basically fit the same mold?"

"Well Frank, to over simplify the situation, yeah, I guess so. That's why we finally came to the conclusion these murders aren't your run of the mill killings. Generally the same type of victim and all killed exactly the same way. This is no fluke. There's a pattern."

"I agree Cal. There are all the signs of being the same person. Let's head down to your office so I can map out some notes from the files. I really need to get all these cases straight in my head before I do anything else."

"Right. Good idea."

"I know it's a good idea. I just said it", I replied as I pushed my chair back and stood. Sidestepping my chair I picked up my cup of coffee while sliding the chair back under the table. Taking my last long gulp Calvin, still across the table from me, followed suit. We set our cups down in unison and I said, "Well, Cal, what say we hit the road?", as I turned around and started toward the door.

"Right behind ya' Frank."

I liked riding around town with Calvin. He always got the best parking spaces. Straight out of the café I crossed the sidewalk to the curb and grabbed the door handle of his sedan and was seated by the time he walked around into the street to get in on the driver side. We were pulling away from the curb as soon as his door made its tell-tale thud when closing. While still accelerating I asked, "Calvin, after all our speculation and theories I haven't asked; has anyone developed any real possibilities in a suspect yet? Any names?"

"Not really. I think some of the other fellas on the squad have come up with a name or two but they're based solely on speculation."

"It's a start."

"As I'm sure when walking in on Mr. McAghon this morning your first thought was 'call girl'. Well, the guys think so too."

"Well at the risk of tarnishing reputations you're right. How else do you get a man face down and naked in bed? I guess the suspect could be a man but let's work this thing out methodically and eliminate the obvious first."

"I'm with you on that. That's one reason I wanted you in on this thing. When you're catching heat from upstairs to solve this thing yesterday and chasing a bunch of Dick Tracys around checking their work you can miss things. You my friend are my extra eyes and ears. Unofficially, this is now your case." Then Calvin slowed his canter down and spoke a little lighter and deliberately saying, "And you should know-"

"What? What should I know?" I interjected with a raised eyebrow.

"One of the victims was a close friend of the mayor. He wants somebody's head and he wants it now. He has personally approved to pay your fees with no questions. You're in the catbird's seat buddy. You have unlimited access to resources to work this thing and you can name your price. What private dick wouldn't want to get a case like this?"

"Yeah. Who wouldn't want this case? Really!? Are you kidding me? You know as well as I do there's going to be some catch somewhere."

"Don't rock the boat with the Mayor's Office Frank. Just take it and let's get started on it, okay?"

"No need to say any more. I know how this stuff works only too well."

"I thought you did."

oOo

We finally got down to Little Italy and the Police Building on Centre Street and Grand. The walk from the Lieutenant's car to his office was much farther than in and out of the diner. The foot traffic in and out of the Police Building's main entrance had already picked up to a brisk pace too for a Sunday. There was never a slow day down there.

"Hey Cal."

"Yeah?"

"If we're still down here later what'd'ya say lunch at Callahan's?"

"You missin' the old days, Frank?"

"Oh, you know how it is. We all do. The Glory Days. You do too and if you say you don't you're lyin'."

"Lunch is still a long way off but alright, I'm in."

It took about another hour to get settled in with the files. Since our newest member of the Dead Club just came on board this morning his file wasn't available. But I did have the other four and they were plenty to deal with. I knew I needed to read through these and make as many notes as I could and do it quick. There were some down here that didn't care for me camping out and I certainly couldn't take the files with me.

It seems our first victim died just before Thanksgiving of last year. Specifically, he was discovered on Monday morning, October 20th, 1939 at about eleven after he failed to show up for work. His name was Samuel Brody, a white male about 37 years old and living alone at 402 5th Avenue. He worked as a plumber uptown. Our next guy was also found on a Sunday, like the guy today, in mid-December. December 17th to be exact. His name was David Coley and he lived at 252 South Street with his mother. He was 29 years old and worked at Wall Street as a clerk. He wasn't at home but rather a suite at the Hotel Commodore when he was killed. Otherwise he was killed the same way. Next up is a chap named James Quarles. He lived alone at 345 East 54th Street. He was also found at the Commodore on Sunday, January 14th making him number one for 1940. Next on deck was an Edward Duncan of 445 East 86th Street. He was another found at home after failing to show for work. That was Monday, February 19th. And finally our newest member of the club, Mr. James McAghon, found today, Sunday, March 17th. Unfortunately it appears Mr. McAghon will be missing the St. Patrick's Day parade this afternoon.

Now all I have to do is figure out why all these men were killed exactly the same way. Why did it start in November with Brody? What is the catalyst that ignited this thing? What could these guys possibly have in common? Some are blue collar men who work at real jobs and others work on Wall Street trading and banking. Why are they always killed in the middle of the month? There is a pattern here but it's still very fuzzy. There has to be a connection. Something they all have in common. But what the hell is it? And who will it point back too. Right now everyone is a suspect and everyone is a potential victim.

After a while I had scratched out copious notes which would require extensive decoding when I got home. I even scrawled out a couple of charts and graphs thinking that would add some clearer picture of this circus. At the moment I was still as stagnant as before. Maybe more so due to the lack of sleep. I was operating more mechanically than mentally. Going through the motions. I would worry about studying this stuff later.

"Hey Calvin", I shouted into the adjacent room.

"What?" came his reply.

By now I had walked from the desk to his office doorway. "Calvin." He looked up from his desk to see me standing there.

"Calvin, I think I'm just going to go home now."

"What? No lunch across the street?"

"No. Not today. I think I've got what I need to start on this case but it's been a really long day."

"I know. I think I'll head home now too", he answered.

Tomorrow would be another day to take a fresh run at this. And pushing myself through the rest of today was not going to help Mr. James McAghon one bit. He was still in a cooler down at 'The Pit' and wasn't likely to leave because of anything I did.

3

Calvin and I both having had a long tedious Sunday decided it was time to head out. Gathering my newly minted files we started back out toward his car. "I just remembered."

"Remembered what?" asked Calvin.

"It's Sunday and I parked near the corner right in front of the church."

"So?"

"So!? It was still dark this morning when I got there and I wasn't looking for restricted parking spaces. I hope I didn't stop in the wrong place and get towed", I said.

"Don't worry. If it's not there I'll go get it out."

"Calvin?"

"What Frank?"

"You're a regular Joe."

"Yeah, yeah; once partners, always partners. You'd do it too."

About now we were in the back lot walking up to his car. "Are you sure about that?"

"Shut up Frank and get in."

Pulling up to the intersection the street was clear of practically any traffic or parked cars. Mine was still there waiting for me. "You mean we were down there long enough for everyone to show up for mass and leave?"

"Yeah, the time snuck up on us", Calvin said while looking at his watch. "It's already two." I'd been in such a blur when I left my place I forgot my watch so I had lost all track of time up until now.

Stepping out into the street between Cal's car and mine I thanked him for the ride back and closed the door. Pulling away, I heard the low throaty sound of his flathead V-8 as I turned to the driver door. Although Calvin's car was a plain unmarked black sedan it had been ordered with the specially tuned police motor. Not much on the road could pull away from it. With after-market suspension tuning they were almost as good as the Harleys in a chase in the city.

Climbing back into my more modest, but new, '39 Chevy coupe I remembered when turning the key and hearing the quieter, smoother sound. No V8 here. Just a 200 cubic inch straight six making about eight-five horses. Since I don't chase anybody, ever, I didn't really care. The only thing that mattered now was it would get me home.

The next morning while at my desk I was poring over all the material from the day before. I had pages of notes and diagrams spread out everywhere. My desk was covered and some pages were strategically placed on other various pieces of furniture. I was just now in a place where I could remotely begin to map it out. Just as I was beginning to immerse myself in constructing a timeline a light rapping sound came from the outer office.

"Hello?" could be lightly heard from the hall. As I walked out of my office toward the door the knobbed turned and the door slowly swung open. I stopped short so as to not let the door hit me and a young lady leaned in while still holding the outside knob. When she did we met there face to face. Startled, she jumped back saying, "Oh my! I'm so sorry. No wait! I'm not sorry. You scared me to death. Who are you!?"

"Who am I? You're kidding, right? This is my office. Who are you sneaking in here like that?"

"Sneaking? I beg your pardon. I'm not sneaking in anywhere. I had an appointment here this morning."

"Oh you did? I don't think so Miss. I'm pretty busy so if you don't mind?"

"Are you Frank DeGrae?" she asked.

Intrigued, I responded slowly with raised eyebrow, "Uh, yeah, I'm Frank."

"Well 'Frank'... you told me on the phone last week to meet with you at this address this morning at 10:00."

I suddenly remembered. With both eyes wide open as if seeing a ghost I jumped back saying, "Oh! Wait! Hold on. Please come in. Don't go" and I ran back to my office. Sliding the papers around on my desk with some finding their way to the floor I found my appointment book. The young lady sauntered in my door from the front office as I looked up from behind the desk.

"Well?" she asked.

"Miss Landers?"

"The gentleman wins a cigar."

"Look, it's been crazy around here for a while and I have to admit, I forgot. I apologize Miss Landers. Would you please come on in and have a seat?"

"Alright", she answered as she continued toward the desk at the same pace. "Are you going to offer me anything to drink?"

"What?"

"Coffee. A cup of coffee Mr. DeGrae."

"Oh. Right. Coffee."

"Never mind."

"Sorry. I don't have any made."

"Fine. Are you alright?" she asked.

"No, I don't think so. I've been running in circles chasing my tail for about a week now. Look Miss Landers, I'm desperate for some help in here. You're hired. When can you start?"

"Hold on there. I think we may need to discuss a few things first."

"Really?"

"I didn't stutter."

Taken aback a bit with her attitude I replied in an unamused tone. With a stone faced expression I responded with, "Now hold on just a minute there missy-"

"No Frank, I will not. I want to put my cards on the table right up front. I want no confusion later down the road."

"Later down the road?"

"You need help and here I am. But know I'm not just a typist and I make coffee because I drink it and want a cup. Not because someone told me to."

"Wait. Who do you think you are ma'am?" came my curt answer to her aggressive tone.

"I don't think. I know exactly who I am. Sir, my name is Sarah Landers. Ring a bell?"

"No. Should it?"

"Does Richard Charles ring a bell?"

I know I once again looked like I had seen a ghost float by. "You're that Sarah Landers?" came my slow and deliberate reply.

"How many do you know?"

"Look Sarah; you don't mind if I call you Sarah do you?"

"Sarah's fine. Frank", she said.

"Okay Sarah. All the pieces are coming together now. I do know who you are. I also know you're quite a bit more than a secretary. Why did you answer my ad? I heard when Charles closed up shop and headed west you followed in his footsteps."

"I did. And still working cases."

"So-"

"I can do the admin work around here with little effort and double as a partner investigator. And your agency has taken on enough work with no growth you're about to get in trouble."

Puzzled at how she knew that, I just scratched my head staring at the floor acknowledging she was right. "So Sarah, you obviously had more on your mind than a simple secretary job when you came in here. What are you proposing?"

"Frank, can I be... frank? Sorry about that. I do crack myself up sometimes."

"Heard it before. Not funny."

"I'm proposing a partnership more than looking for a job. In fact, I don't need the job but I know how good you are and combined I feel we could lock New York down."

"I need to think about this Sarah. I know some of the things you pulled off for Rick and I know you know this game but I wasn't exactly thinking about this sort of thing. Not until now anyway."

With that she stood, picked up her pocketbook, and started for the door. As I just stood there watching her walk away she said, "Alright Frank. When you realize you need me give me a call. But don't wait too long. This offer has an expiration date."

"So Sarah-" She stopped at the door and looked back. "What is the expiration date?"

"You'll know", and she turned back toward the door, walked across the front office, and left. I admit my interest was piqued.

Rick had been gone for years and I really didn't know where he was these days but I had plenty of other avenues to check up on Miss Landers. Suddenly these murders took a back seat to what I needed to do right now. I desperately needed some help. Sarah was right. My case load had almost grown beyond what I could handle and since the Mayor had a personal interest in this latest one and wanted it solved yesterday the heat had been turned up. I almost hated to admit it but she is either very good or her timing was really good luck. And I don't much believe in luck. Since I know she worked for Charles and was still working in the gumshoe racket I don't think luck had much to do with it at all.

oOo

Just sitting behind my desk doing nothing; papers scattered everywhere like confetti on Fifth Avenue after a St. Patrick's Day Parade, I picked up the horn and called

Akers' office. When I dialed the last number I reached for the pack of Camels on the desk.

Having just lit the cigarette, "Police Building. How may I direct your call?" came the voice of the PBX operator.

"Yes ma'am. Is Lieutenant Calvin Akers in?"

"May I say who is calling?"

"Frank DeGrae."

"Hold please", she said and then the line went dead. Or so it sounded after a click. After a short wait I heard the click again followed by, "Hold please while I redirect your call", followed by another click.

After quite a long pause came, "Hey Frank, how's it goin'?" after one more click of the phone connections.

"Calvin, you busy?"

"Now what do you think?"

"Look Cal, I need a quick check on a Sarah Landers. You might know her, or at least remember her. I think she's a shamus working here in New York."

"Oh really?" he replied with a long drawn out voice of disbelief. "A gumshoe you say? A lady dick? What next Frank?"

"She was Richard Charles' secretary before he blew town for California. Now do you remember?"

"Oh... wait a minute now."

"Yeah Cal. Her."

"Yeah Frank, I think I do now. Right, I think she is still in New York."

"I really need somebody to get her story. Is she a private dick and anything else on her? I'm thinking of calling her in on this serial thing if she pans out."

"I'm on it Frank. I'll call you back in a few", Akers said as he hung up. Apparently when he knew I needed her for his serial killer he didn't hesitate.

While moving to hang the phone back in its cradle I paused and gazed at it. I decided to ring up the mayor's office. There were a couple of small details I wanted to cover with him and now was as good a time as any.

After several minutes and being passed around to half the ladies working in City Hall I finally got as far as the Mayor's receptionist. I never spoke with the Mayor but his Administrative Assistant did book an appointment for me to come by this afternoon. That was even better.

It was coming up on lunch time so I decided to head out and make the rounds on the way down there. Since I'd been on the blower all morning I didn't know if Calvin had tried to call back. Rather than wasting more time on the phone I decided to drop in on him on the way to City Hall Park.

Since I live only three blocks from my office I walk to work most days as was the case today. After locking up I took the elevator down and left the building out to 5th Avenue and walked around the corner to East 57th Street. The weather was perfect and the traffic was horrendous as usual. Another reason I didn't drive unless absolutely necessary. I could also stop about half way home and grab a couple of Nathan's dogs from the sidewalk vendor. For about two bits I was set for the rest of the day.

Arriving at my hotel at the corner of 57th and Lexington I finished off the last bite and pulled open the lobby door. Walking in the 57th Street side I veered off to the left and made my way to the front desk.

"Good afternoon Mr. DeGrae", the desk clerk offered as he turned his back to me and retrieved my mail from its pigeon hole.

"How's it going Billy?"

Turning back to hand me my mail he answered, "Can't be better Mr. DeGrae. Thanks. Can I get you anything else today?"

"Oh, no Billy. Thanks", I said as I turned toward the elevators and shuffled through the envelopes as if they were a winning poker hand. They weren't. They were bills. They're always bills.

A quick stop at the apartment and I was on the fly again. Walking back out onto Lexington I strolled down to the parking garage and found my car. With the midday lunch break winding down the pedestrian and vehicle traffic was almost more than you could take. Everyone was trying to get somewhere.

I would need the car now since my trip to City Hall was substantially more than three blocks away. The good thing about dropping in on Cal was the Police Building was on the way.

Taking Lexington down to Gramercy Park before detouring over to 3rd Avenue I pretty much followed the el down through the Bowery where I could turn onto Grand and make it to the Police Building. It seemed to be the shortest route from my place down to Calvin's office.

Parking on the back side of the building I managed to get inside a bit quicker. I thought I would just take the lobby stairs up since his office was only one floor up but when I got to Investigations no one was there. It seemed I was in a big rush for no reason. When I walked in the front office secretary looked up from her work and asked, "Yes sir? May I help you?" and quickly changed gears when I came into focus with, "Oh, it's just you. Hi Frank. He's not back yet."

"Yeah Vicky, it's just me. Thanks. Where is he?"

"Oh, he just stepped across the street for lunch. He should be back just anytime. Go on in and have a seat while you wait."

Walking across the front of her desk toward Calvin's door I said, "Thanks" as I grabbed the doorknob.

It wasn't long before Akers showed up. Before he could step completely in and get the door shut Calvin was all smiles with, "Well hey Frank. How's it going?" followed by the thud of the door closing and latching. He was apparently warned I was here.

"Fine Cal, just fine. Look, I'm on my way down to the Mayor's Office and thought I'd check in to see if we know anything more about Sarah. After we talked this morning I pretty much kept the phone tied up so I didn't know if you tried to call back."

"Yeah Frank. She's what she claims. It was an easy check of some city records. She has a P.I. license and business license. You can bring her aboard if you want to work with her."

"Good. That's why I'm heading down to City Hall Park when I leave. I have an appointment to meet with the Mayor this afternoon to run this by him."

"Oh?"

"Yeah. He's going to pay her fees too."

"Oh he is?" Akers asked.

"I'm not. And I would wager you won't"

"You're right about that. She probably charges about what you do and I know it's not in my budget."

"Bingo. I can't afford to pay me either."

"Oh, I almost forgot Frank, the file packet on McAghon is pretty much complete now. You can copy it now if you want to put it with the rest. We're just waiting for the official medical examiner report."

"Great. I'll try to swing back around tomorrow for it. I need to get on down to the Mayor's office now. And that reminds me. Did you go over to Callahan's for lunch?"

"Well, yeah, I did."

"Go again without me and there'll be a reckonin'"

"It's just across the street Frank. What do you expect?"

"I expect I'll be back for the file tomorrow and we're going for lunch over there."

"Fine Frank. We're going to Callahan's tomorrow. Now get out of here. You need to schmooze with the Mayor and con more money out of him and I've got some real work to do."

"Right Cal. If you call this working."

4

When I got down to City Hall I had completely forgotten about the wreckage of the renovation. Navigating around the City Hall Park area and finding parking was not going to be easy. After nearly two years the razing of the Post Office and Courts building to clear the corner park area was still causing mayhem for traffic. I was glad I decided to come on down a little early.

After more than twenty minutes I finally just parked on the street behind City Hall. I thought it should be alright since it wasn't near traffic or blocking any trolley tracks. When I walked up the front steps it was still only 3:30 so I was still making good time. The last thing I wanted to do was irritate the Mayor having to sit around waiting on me. Then again, I don't think he would do that. If I ran late I would just miss him.

Entering the main hall I walked to the center reception area and arriving at the counter I said, "Excuse me ma'am. Ma'am?" One of the ladies finally turned and looked in my direction. Thinking I was about to engage in conversation she turned her attention back to what she had been doing.

"Excuse me ma'am but I have an appointment to meet with Mayor La Guardia at four. Could someone announce me please?"

With that pronouncement everyone at the station stopped and looked at me. All things considered, the hall seemed to grow quiet. One lady walked over to me and replied, "Excuse me sir. Did you say you have a scheduled appointment with the Mayor this afternoon?"

"I did indeed. Could you so kindly call up and let them know I'm here?"

"Your name sir?"

"DeGrae. Mr. Francis DeGrae. He's expecting me."

"One moment Mr. DeGrae", she said as she walked back to a desk with a large PBX exchange mounted on it. She sat down and placed earphones on her head and jammed a large metallic plug into one of the seemingly hundreds of receptacles. Various lights could be seen coming on and going off on the console and you could tell she was speaking but could not be understood; her voice was subdued and muffled by other ambient noises in the great hall. After a moment she pulled the plug out of the wall and removed her headset. Walking back to me she offered, "Mr. DeGrae, if you would take elevator 4", while pointing toward a bank of elevators to my left, "to the top floor, go left when you step off, and stop in the center of the hall at another reception area they will direct you to his office."

"Thank you kindly for all of your assistance ma'am. It's much appreciated", I said to her as I turned and made for the elevators. All elevator doors were closed and the gauge above the door indicated mine was already at the top floor. It seems everyone in New York is always in a hurry and at the same time you can't get anywhere fast.

My mind now preoccupied with studying the architecture and artwork came the loud 'ding' of the car's bell and the rattling of the manual sliding scissor gate at the hands of the operator while the exterior door retracted into the wall. I was jolted back to reality and remained standing slightly to one side in the event there were passengers needing to disembark. Oddly there were none. I stepped aboard.

Stepping to the back of the car all I said as I turned back around was, "Mayor's Office please." With no verbal response the elevator operator simply pulled the gate closed. As the outer door completely shut he toggled the lever to the right. The car slowly began to climb.

After a short ascent the operator manipulated the lever slightly and the car gradually slowed until stopping at the correct position. When stopped he once again grabbed a handle on the gate and pulled it open. With the door open I was once again given directions to the Mayor's Office.

Stepping out into the hallway my eye immediately caught a continuation of the fanciful architecture and works of art adorning the walls. The City Hall was an art museum in its own right. Focusing on the mission at hand I continued down the hall to the next reception area.

"Hello ladies", and all heads turned toward me. "I'm Frank DeGrae. The Mayor's expecting me."

With no more phone calls or delays one woman immediately approached me with her hand extended saying, "Right this way Mr. DeGrae. We've been expecting you", as she stepped around to my side of the barricade. I followed her around the dais after she stepped down and shook my hand. A few more steps and we were there. This reminded me of finally getting to see the wizard in Emerald City.

"He will see you now", she said to me as she partially opened an office door that stretched from floor to ceiling and stepped away. I continued opening the heavy yet balanced and easy to open door and entered the office. Stepping in and pulling the door closed behind me I heard, "Well, Mr. DeGrae, I presume? Welcome. Have a seat."

I looked back around from closing the massive and ornately carved solid oak door to see the man standing behind a desk. There were the usual trappings of accent furniture, small statues, and various framed artwork of nothing in particular adorning the walls. This office, however, seemed to be about twice the size one would expect even of the Mayor's office. And he had his own fireplace. No doubt a holdover from earlier days when such a luxury was in fact a necessity. After all the building has been in use for well over a hundred years.

The man himself did not appear to be anything out of the ordinary. Not particularly imposing yet there was no doubt of his confidence. He was a man you knew was in charge of his world. Of average height and a bit over-weight he was well dressed but exuded friendship and goodwill along with no-nonsense professionalism. This was a man who dealt harshly with adversaries and had a heart to help his fellow man. I was in the company of a statesman.

"Yes, Mr. Mayor. I'm Frank DeGrae and thank you for taking the time to see me this afternoon", I replied as I placed my hat on a small, but ornate, accent table next to the door and walked toward the desk. Approaching, I extended my hand to greet him.

Standing across from one another shaking hands he then gestured with the same open hand followed with, "Please, have a seat."

"Thank you sir", I answered as I settled into one of the two very large and inviting heavy leather throne-like chairs stationed in front of his desk. I had never seen the White House Oval Office but it surely couldn't be much nicer than this.

"Can I get you anything Mr. DeGrae? Something to drink? Coffee perhaps?"

"Oh no. Thank you sir. I won't be but a minute. I know how busy you are and I don't want to keep you any longer than is necessary."

"The work day is over sir. There's no need to rush", he said as he reached for the intercom on his desk. Pushing a small toggle down and speaking again, "Dorothy? Could you have someone bring in some coffee?"

"Yes sir", came a voice from the console.

"Sir, there were just a couple of small matters I wanted to go over with you concerning this situation we have that is starting to look like a serial killer in the city."

"And I as well with you Mr. DeGrae", replied the Mayor. "I'm glad you called to arrange this meeting. It saved me the trouble."

That was unexpected. "Oh? Do tell."

"Frank- may I call you Frank? I actually hate formalities in settings such as this."

"Uh, well yes. Yes sir. Please do."

"Well Frank, I have a few things of a sensitive nature I wanted to run by you we think could also be connected and get your take. Don't worry, you've been vetted and cleared to hear whatever I'm about to tell you."

"I see."

"I've been briefed on you. I know you served in the Army during the Great War, as did I, and you joined the NYPD not long afterward. I know you left the department after a few years but your service was honorable and you still maintain close friendships with active officers. And you come with high recommendations as a private investigator licensed here in the city. In short, you can be trusted."

"Yes sir, I suppose your briefing was accurate. All my work is kept in the strictest confidence."

"Well some of the things I'm going to tell you will extend well beyond keeping private secrets. It may include matters of criminal activity and even matters of national security."

"National security?"

"Yes Frank. National security. I'm sure as busy as you are, you've also been keeping up with current events."

"Yes."

"Although we here in the United States are still enjoying a peace-time existence a great war has started in most of the rest of the world. Some say it's only a matter of time before we're dragged into it. Asia has been embroiled in armed conflict for years and Hitler kicked off war in Europe last year."

"Yes sir. I've been reading the papers."

"Well what you may not know because it is not being covered by the media is it's believed a fairly large and well organized spy ring is operating along our East Coast. And they've set up their base of operations here, in New York City."

"Are you serious?"

"This information has come to me from the Governor's office and the New York Attorney General's office in co-operation with the US Attorney's Office here in New York and FBI director J. Edgar Hoover. Hoover's local man is a Special Agent Jim Ellison."

"How does all this involve me?"

"Frank- no one knows yet anything about these murders you're working on with Lieutenant Akers and it may turn out there is no connection at all but-"

"Yes?"

"Your most recent victim, Mr. James McAghon, was an FBI informant here on the ground. We don't know if his murder has anything to do with this spy ring or his personal demons."

"Personal demons?"

"Well, you'll find out on your own he was no angel either in his private affairs. Those matters are really none of my concern. But you needed to be made aware of the deep waters you're about to wade into. If for no other reason your own personal safety may be at risk. And if some of this does hit you in the face you're to take no action other than to report back what you know. Hoover's men are on this."

"Understood."

"Frank, the confidentiality of all this is of the strictest nature. You cannot mention any of this conversation to anyone. This is of the highest national security concerns. Should anything get out the efforts to reign them in will be grossly compromised and may even endanger the lives of our guys. I know you're a patriot and military veteran understanding exactly what this means."

"Yes sir. Understood."

About now came a knock at the door followed by it swinging open. I turned in my chair and we both watched as a serving tray followed by a lovely young lady enter the room. "Your coffee, sir."

"Thank you Dorothy."

She added, "I'm so sorry it took so long. Since it was so late in the afternoon we made a fresh pot. If we left anything out- if there's anything else you need just let me know."

"Thank you Dorothy. It looks fine. You can set it on the table there", he said while pointing to a small serving cart standing between my chair and its mate. After placing the well-stocked and ornate Tiffany sterling silver six piece tea and coffee service on the table Dorothy made her way back out.

As the Mayor rose from his chair he said, "Go ahead Frank, help yourself", and continued walking from behind the desk.

I rose from my chair and picked up a cup. "Thank you sir, I believe I will." I picked up a second cup and turned to hand it to him. After we filled our cups and doctored the brew we sat back down. This time he occupied the other chair across the serving cart from me.

"Now Frank, what was it you wanted to talk to me about?"

"Well, it goes back to the actual murder cases the police department is working on. I've had an opportunity to more or less get up to speed on them. We're now up to five possible related cases and the truth is I'm getting backed up."

"You need help?"

"Well actually, I could use an extra pair of helping hands. Yes."

"You've got it."

"Well thanks but it's really a matter of money. I have a partner in mind but her salary will need to be met."

"If you have someone in mind I trust your judgement. Bring this person onboard and submit your invoices."

"That was easy. Thanks."

"Did you say 'her'?"

"I did. Do you remember when Richard Charles was here?"

"Of course."

"Well when he was working here he had a real bang-up secretary by the name of Sarah Landers. I mean she really knows her onions and had connections you wouldn't believe."

"Go on."

"Behind the scenes on his last big case here before moving to San Francisco I think she did almost as much to wrap it up as he did. Anyway, she turned down relocating with him and took up sleuthing on her own. Akers has checked her out and she does have current P.I. and business licenses to operate here in the city."

"Have you talked with her about this yet?"

"That's the funny thing Mr. Mayor, she somehow picked up on the situation and contacted me. She's offered to partner with me to work this thing but I didn't know how she would be paid for her time. Not until now anyway. We haven't struck a deal yet but I'll call her tomorrow to get this thing rolling."

"That's fine Frank. You just submit your bill like we've already set it up and add her salary to it. You'll pay her. I don't want to upset the apple cart running this through all the bureaucracy. It'll just slow things down. But as far as the dollar amount goes, consider it approved."

"Thank you Mr. Mayor. I guess that wraps things up then. At least for now."

When the Mayor stood from his chair I took the hint and figured our business was concluded. As he placed his cup back on the tray I stood and we shook hands. "Thank you sir for seeing me today."

"It was my pleasure Frank. Thanks for coming onboard with all this. Don't hesitate to drop back in and let me know if there's anything else you need."

"I won't. Thanks", I replied as I stepped around and retrieved my hat.

5

I skipped dropping by the office altogether and drove straight down to the Police Building when I left my apartment this morning. Since it was so early when I got there I parked and walked in on the front side. Once in the main lobby I made a beeline to the information desk. "Is Akers in his office yet Judy?"

Looking up from filing her nails, and smacking her chewing gum, she replied with, "Oh, hi Frank. How ya' been? You never come 'round anymoa'."

"I've gotten much busier since I left sweetheart. No time for anything anymore."

"That's too bad Frank. I can still think of a couple a' things to do."

"I just bet you can honey. Can we put the reminiscing on hold? I really need to see Akers."

"Hang on stud and I'll call up", she said with a slightly pushed out crooked lip and one raised brow feigning desire and disappointment. "He neva' comes in the front so I wouldn't know unless I called", now over accentuating her Betty Boop pitch.

"Don't let me stop you", I answered as she picked up the phone.

Looking around the foyer I was taking in architectural details I've never noticed before when Judy barked in her Brooklyn inflection, "Yeah Frank. He's in."

Starting around her station for the stairs I said, "Thanks Judy. See ya' later."

"Yeah Frank. Promises, promises."

Traversing the stairs to the next floor, a quick left turn, and another left three doors down I was walking in calling out to Calvin. "Frank. Back here" Calvin answered.

As I entered Calvin's rear office I said, "I got in to see the Mayor yesterday afternoon", as I hung my hat on the coat tree. Turning back toward his desk I continued with, "It looks like everything is on the ready now."

"Really? He approved to pay you more money?"

"With no hesitation. I'll be calling Sarah later this morning and bring her up to speed. What I really came by for was to get a copy of the McAghon M.E. report if you have it. Maybe I can get all these cases reconciled in my head and start the sifting now."

Picking up a beige legal length file folder from his desk and extended his arm in my direction Calvin said, "Well pal, here it is. Knock yourself out while I start some coffee."

I reached out and took it and he strolled back up front to assemble the apparatus that would yield the nectar of the Columbian gods. I got to work.

"Hey, Cal?" I called out to other room.

"Yeah?"

"Was that apartment at 55 Central Park West his?"

"McAghon's?"

"Uh, Yeah Cal. McAghon's. That is the dead guy, right?"

Walking back through the door he also replied, "Wise guy, huh? Yes Frank, McAghon is the dead guy and it was his apartment. Why?"

"Do we know what he did? How did he make his money?" I was curious how much Calvin knew about our guy but I wasn't giving anything I learned from the Mayor.

"I think he worked down on Wall Street. It should be in the file there somewhere", he said as he walked back to the desk. Reaching out for the folder I handed it back to him. "Here", he said with his finger touching a typed-in line near the top while rotating the folder around for me to see. Below McAghon's typed name and address was a line simply identified as 'P.O.E.'. It showed he worked at the

New York Stock Exchange at the main building located at #
11 Wall Street.

"That's fine Calvin but what did he do?"

"Do I have to do everything? Go down there and find
out."

"Fine", I said as I stood from behind the desk. I guess
he wanted his chair back. Closing the folder and tucking it
under my left arm I said, "It's just below City Hall.
Shouldn't take more than a few minutes to get down
there."

"Good", replied Calvin as he moved around the desk to
fill the void I had left. "I've got plenty to do around here
without you under foot", he finished as he sat down.

"If I didn't know better I'd think you wanted me
gone."

"Go already!"

Already at the door putting my hat on I couldn't help
but mix a little chuckle in with, "You're gonna' miss me."

"Are you still here?"

"No." And I walked out into the hall.

oOo

When I got down to the Financial District I located 11
Wall Street quickly but it wasn't long until I realized it was
going to be an exercise in patience trying to locate an
employee down here. The FiDi, and especially the
Exchange, was more than just a building or two. It's a city
within the city. There were so many people and so much
activity the place gave the appearance of more of a
machine running than a group of working people. It was a
factory that churned out long thin slips of paper. The
sprockets and cogs were people yelling frantically and
flailing their arms about. None of it made sense to me.

As it turned out our Mr. James McAghon worked for a
small, virtually unknown broker who dealt primarily with
trading government bonds. The depression was still
lingering and no stocks were being traded on margins

anymore. Everything traded was strictly cash on the barrel head. Credit was a thing of the past. Roosevelt's 'New Deal' had clamped down hard on the game playing at Wall Street. The question now was how did a thirty-three year old low level bond salesman manage to afford living at 55 Central Park West?

6

Once I figured out a little more about our boy I decided to check back with the fellas working the case from the other side. This thing had way too many irons in the fire. A full-on free-for-all party involving everyone from Federal, State, Local, and private concerns. There's no doubt there is work being duplicated and secrets held from one another. This sort of cross-over thing is always victim to this. Nonetheless I was headed to see our Special Agent Ellison. I figured I wouldn't get far but I had to check it out.

Heading back uptown from City Hall I decided to make a stop at 'The Pit'. I figured I'd be spinning my wheels but curiosity got the better of me.

Walking in the service entrance I spotted Anne. "Hey, where's Tommy?"

Slightly startled and snapping her head around she said, "Oh, it's just you."

"Sorry to disappoint."

"Yeah, sure you are. He's back there where he always is."

"Thanks", I said as I passed.

As I made my way from a business like atmosphere of an office intake area down a long dim hallway I could hear the faint sounds of lab work. Nothing remarkable, yet still very creepy. I stopped at the door where the sound seemed most pronounced. I lightly tapped on the oak door with my right index finger knuckle.

"Yeah", was heard from the other side. I clutched the door knob, turned it, and slowly pushed the door.

"Tommy?"

Before the door was open far enough to see in I heard, "Oh, Frank. Come on in."

Stepping into the inner sanctum of 'The Pit' I could only see someone standing with their back to me leaning over a waist high examination table. Beyond was the exterior wall made up mostly of large transomed windows that were canted open allowing the room to fill with natural light and the odor to escape. The remaining walls were home to shelves of books and specimen jars. The high slatted ceiling was home to one large slow moving fan. This, no doubt, helped facilitate moving out the formaldehyde and pulling in fresh air. Someone was lying on the table but I didn't know who it was.

"So, who's your customer today?" I asked.

"Oh, this is nobody. What brings you down?" he said, turning away from the table.

As Tommy stepped away from his patient and began pulling off his lab coat I started with, "Well I thought I'd drop in and check on our latest scissors victim."

"I should have known."

"Well?"

He continued with, "Not much. Pretty much the same as the others. No other wounds, in good health, and no sign of a struggle or intoxication."

"So all these guys were just lying in bed waiting to be stabbed in the back?"

"Apparently so."

"How would one manage to arrange that set-up?" I asked.

"I have no idea. That's your problem to figure out."

I just nodded at that when he followed up with, "Oh, I almost forgot."

"What?"

"Yesterday. Yesterday a woman came around asking about him."

"Oh?"

"Yeah. His name is McAghon, right?"

"Right. James McAghon. Get her name?"

"That's what I thought. You know we have so many come through here I have trouble remembering names."

"Did you get her name!?" I repeated.

"No. And yes, we asked. We told her we didn't know anything yet and asked for her information so we could call her back. She just said she would come back and hit the door."

"Thanks. What did she look like?"

Our conversation went on for quite some time and when I left I spoke to Anne out front about our mystery lady for a while too. I didn't have much to go on but enough to have a sit down with Ellison. I was sure with his help we could put a name and face together who knew McAghon. Or at least I was hoping we could.

I decided to go over the files again so I went back to my office. I know I've missed something but what it was, was anyone's guess. It's usually something simple. Something staring you right in the face and so obvious it's overlooked. I needed a fresh approach. A new set of eyes to look at this. I needed to call Sarah.

7

Sitting in an accent chair between my filing cabinet and barrister I was using the natural light shining through the window to study McAghon's file. Then my concentration was broken by a rap at the door.

"Yes", I called out. With no reply the door knob slowly turned. I moved from the window while pulling my gun from its shoulder holster. As I moved for cover behind the desk the door slowly opened further.

"Mr. DeGrae?"

"Sarah?" Still unable to see her; "Is that you?"

As the door opened fully and she came into view she answered, "Yes. Can you give me a hand here?"

I re-holstered as I walked toward the door. "What are you doing?"

"You're a detective. What do you think?" She asked.

It was now quite obvious she was heavily encumbered with a large purse, tote bag with file folders, cups of coffee in a paperboard carrier and a box of doughnuts.

"Here, give me something", I said as I reached out toward her.

Without hesitation came, "Just grab anything before it hits the floor."

"Anything?"

Everything going on stopped. The scene was frozen in time other than the cold stare. "You know what I mean. Don't look that way", I said.

"I know what you mean and if there are any more of those locker room shots I'm walking. And that's after I deck you. I'm not one of your girls."

"Alright. Sorry. Let's get this stuff settled and get some work done. I found something I want you to see and get a fresh perspective on it."

I grabbed the coffee and doughnuts since they were closest to dropping from Sarah's grip. And of course I took a shot from her for that too. I just took it and walked toward a table against the adjacent wall. I was learning this one was going to be a force to reckon with and another practical example of 'choose your battles'.

As I placed the coffee and doughnut box at one end of the work table I heard a thud and abruptly turned to look back at Sarah. I observed her large handbag was on the floor near her left foot as she placed the large portable file cabinet on her end of the table.

"What is that stuff?" I asked.

"Wouldn't you like to know? Let's see your stuff first and then I'll show you what I dug up."

I turned toward the desk as I answered and picked up the file folder. "This", I said as I raised the folder and turned back around to face her. She hadn't moved but was standing with her back to me picking up a doughnut with a napkin as she held her paper cup of black coffee.

"Miss Landers."

Still situating her doughnut just so in the napkin she answered, still with her back to me, "Yes?"

"Miss Landers?"

"Go ahead Frank. I don't read lips. I can hear without looking at you."

I thought here we go again. "Were you ever a cop?"

"What?"

"I was just guessing. You've got the mouth to match one."

"Why thank you Frank. That's the nicest thing anyone ever said to me. Are you through wasting time and ready to get some work done?"

"Where did you get this stuff?" I asked.

"I can't give away all my secrets. For now you'll have to trust me", Sarah replied.

Looking at the header tabs on the file folders I said, "Seriously, how did you get these files on these people? This is classified information. A matter of national security."

"And how do you know this?"

"I don't. Not officially anyway."

"Neither do I. So there. If you have high sources and are keeping things from me then it's a two-way street my friend."

"Ok. You're right. Either we're pooling our resources and working together or we're not. I get it. We can't keep going like this way or we'll never get anything done."

"For once you're talking sense."

"Then tell me about those files", I said.

"Nice try. I at least showed the files. You bring me up to speed on what you have. All of it or we're done. And I'll shore up these."

"Fair enough", I said. "What I'm about to tell you I got from the Mayor's Office and then the local FBI Field Office. If any of this gets out there will be hell to pay. Maybe jail. Capeesh?"

"Capeesh. Now give."

"Sit down", I said as I followed my own advice. Sarah walked over and sat down opposite me in front of the desk. "For starters, our man McAghon appears to be, or have links to, a Nazi spy. Maybe even more than one. They're still working that one out right now."

"Really?"

"I'm not kidding. I got this from meeting with the mayor."

"Go ahead. I'm sorry."

"Thank you. Anyway, this McAghon fellow was working with the local FBI Special Agent in-charge Jim Ellison. I met with Jim a short time after my meeting with the mayor. It seems McAghon was on the FBI payroll as an informant or double agent or something like that. I'm not sure."

"Okay."

"Anyway, it turns out the Feds are watching a group of suspected Nazi spies here in New York and it appears there's a link between them and McAghon."

"You've got to be joking."

"I wish I were. Now you must not mention one word of this to anyone. Anyone!"

"Alright. I get it. You'd have to be crazy to blab this around", she finished.

"Yes you would. If it gets out we have this angle it could very well get us held up or we could even disappear. As far as I know even the cops don't know this spy thing about our man."

"Really?"

"I've been back to see Lieutenant Akers a couple of times since finding this out and it has never once come up in conversation. And Akers is getting desperate to solve the murder cases. So I know if he was aware of Agent Ellison's connection he would have mentioned it", I said. "Besides that, Akers and I used to be partners on the street a while back so I know he trusts me with anything he has. I haven't mentioned what I know to him because I was explicitly told by the mayor and Ellison this is a top secret national security matter and to keep it close to my vest. I figured if Akers doesn't know he's better off for it. At least for now."

"And now I know", Sarah followed up.

"And now you know. So we'll use this information together to work this thing but take it to the grave. Get it?"

"Oh yes, I've got it Frank", Sarah said as she raised the cup to try the coffee. Bringing the cup down she followed up with, "So, shall we get to work?"

8

"I've been reading through these for hours. I'm not seeing it", I said.

"Seeing what", Sarah asked.

"The connection! The connection. I know there's one but what is it?"

Calmly she replied, "Now just put it down and walk away."

"What?"

"You heard me. It's time to take a break. Right now you couldn't see my hand slap your face. You've been at it for so long and with such attention you can't see the nuances you need to. Now you're rushing it."

"You are good. And you're right", I said as I tossed the file on the desk. I stood up and walked toward the door grabbing my coat and hat from their hooks. "I'm going downstairs. You need anything?"

"Hold on. I'll go with you", she answered as she also stood and headed toward me. Never slowing her gait as she grabbed her purse from the table and approaching the door I was holding, walked past and said, "Let's go."

Stepping off the elevator into the lobby Sarah slowed and craned her neck looking around. "So, where's the coffee shop?"

"I'm going outside to Nathan's stand."

"You're kidding, right? Hotdogs?"

"That's where I'm headed. You can have whatever you like."

"Good grief", followed and so did she. I also noticed a young man sitting casually in the lobby reading a newspaper. I recognized him from the day before down here but I never saw him before then. Sarah and I walked the long way across the lobby to reach the 57th Street exit rather than go out the 5th Avenue doors. This gave me the opportunity to see our guy better. And he did get up and head toward the doors as we went outside.

"Look Sarah, I don't have long so listen."

"Okay."

"I think we have a tail. He's about to come out the door right behind us. You walk up 57th and I'll walk toward my apartment."

"Right", she answered and no sooner did we split he stepped outside. It was easy to get lost in the moving crowd so I ducked into a covered doorway just a short distance away. He was craning his neck trying to see a couple walking together but there wasn't one in sight. I, on the other hand, had him in my sights. After a while he gave up and started to walk away. It was now my turn to do the following.

I followed our man down 57th until reaching my apartment. As the crowds continued moving up and down the sidewalk I saw him from a distance vanish from sight. He had decided to go ahead and enter my building. Now he was going to stake out the lobby there. At this point I had no doubt he was my shadow. I was going to have to wait him out.

The next morning around 10:00 I made it back into the office. I thought I'd call Sarah to let her know how the evening went after she left. After a few rings she came on the line.

"Hello."

"Sarah. Good morning. Frank."

"Well, how did it go?"

"I've got a tag number. I'm going down to see Cal and find out who this character is. After he left the office building he camped out most of the night in my lobby."

"At your apartment?"

"That's right. At home. This guy is definitely scoping me out. But I'm about to find out why. You keep doing your thing and I'll talk to you later."

"Alright. Thanks. And be careful", she said.

"I didn't know you cared."

"I don't. I just want to make sure I get paid. Bye."

oOo

Not taking any chances on that cock-eyed shaver following me again I took the elevator down to the second floor and let it go on down to the lobby empty. From here I took the stairwell to the outside fire escape and used it to get down to the street. The counterbalanced metal stairs eased me down into the alley and I made a clean escape. He probably sat reading his newspaper all day.

It wasn't long before I made my way to the Police Building. Although it was almost midday I managed to call Calvin before leaving home so I knew he was there. I had to park in the rear of the building but it wasn't a problem. In fact, some of the people were starting to leave for lunch so some parking spaces were opening up.

After I finally got parked and walked around a bit I decided I really did shake off my shadow and no one knew I was here. I guess whoever this fella is he's not at the top of his game. I finally went in the back entrance and back up to see Vicky. She announced me and in I went.

Walking back into Cal's office I was met with the usual, "Well hello Frank. I see you're dragging out of bed late again."

"Very funny. I was only up all day yesterday and all night trying to ID a tail."

"Really? Someone interested in your comings and goings?"

"It would seem. I finally got the guy matched to a car so here's the number. Do your magic and tell us who he is."

Akers took the slip of paper as he stood and looked at it for a moment. "What kind of car was this on Frank?"

"Looked like a new Buick coupe. Black. Nice car. Why?"

"This tag. 3J12*21 looks like an old series. If my guess is right it's a '38 tag and expired. If so, we're gonna' be out of luck."

"Expired? On a new '40 model car?"

"Frank, you know how they're doing these tags. They use the same color scheme of yellow letters on a black tag every other year. And the same black letters on yellow the other years. In the dark, at night, a 1938 tag and 1940 tag look the same. They both even have 'New York World's Fair' written across the bottom. I just remember the sequences and I'm guessing it's a '38. We'll see."

"You're right. I see what you're saying. Well, let's give it a shot. It's all we have right now."

"I'll call when I get anything back", Cal said as he walked toward the door. "I've got to run upstairs to the Chief's office now", he continued as he put on his jacket and hat.

"Right. I've some errands to run too. See ya' later", I said pushing out into the hall ahead of him.

9

While I was down there I decided to go up to Records and pull McAghon's jacket. If he had one. After all this time mulling over these files it finally struck me we haven't looked at the victims' criminal histories. I remember Akers told me he remembered an assault in McAghon's file but nothing much else. I needed to take a look for myself. Sarah was right and I knew it too. You can get tunnel vision and start missing pieces of the puzzle.

Stepping off the elevator I made the right turn and there was the window. Nothing had changed up there. Buffed tile floors with polished marble block walls, all of which were of a medium drab gray. The click-clack hammering sound of typewriters filled the air even out in the hall. One of the girls saw me standing there and yelled out, "Just a moment, sir", and went back to her phone call. The other ladies were typing or standing at filing cabinets. Busy as little bees, they were.

While waiting I was blindsided by another young lady I hadn't even seen in the mix. "Hi Frank, what brings you down here?"

"Hi Mary Kay. I didn't know you were working here now."

"Nothing stays the same you know. So what do you need?"

"Look, I'm working on this string of murders with Akers now. Could you be a dear and pull a 'CH' file for me?"

"Anything for you Frank. Give me a name."

"His name is James McAghon. Here, let me jot it down for you", I said as I took out my pen and turned a notepad around on the counter.

"Oh, I heard about him", she said.

I stopped writing and looked up. "Oh, you did? Do tell."

"Well we all heard about him gettin' killed and all. So Clara remembered when he came through and we started sayin' how funny it was."

"How funny what was?"

"You know, how he killed his wife and now him gettin' killed. I guess there is karma, or whatever it is."

"Really. I didn't know that. Can I see the file? I'd really like to read up on that if I could."

"Sure Frank. Hang on and I'll go grab it."

I guess Calvin didn't read the file after all. I mean, sure he scanned over it real quick and picked up the arrest for assault but apparently he somehow glossed over that McAghon's wife died.

"Here Frank. This is what you're looking for."

"Thanks sweetheart. Can I borrow this for a while?"

"Since he's not going to court now I guess it'll be ok. But please bring it back soon anyway", she said.

I asked, "There was a pending court date?"

"Oh yeah, he just had an arraignment not long ago. Plead Not Guilty and posted a bond. I guess he's not worried about the bond money now, huh?"

"You're a real comedienne. I guess he's not. Thanks for the info. I'll see you soon", I said to her as I turned from the window and starting looking into the folder while slowly moving back toward the elevators.

"Bye Frank. Don't be a stranger", I heard behind me as I continued walking. I raised my left hand in a sort of goodbye wave.

When I got back to the main lobby I went straight to the bank of payphones near the entrance. I had to get hold of Sarah and see what she'd uncovered. I wanted her slant on this murder thing too of McAghon's wife.

"Hello. DeGrae's Private Investigations."

"Sarah? Frank."

"Oh Frank. Hi. Get anything new?"

"Have I. Glad I caught you there. I'm leaving the Police Building and should be there within the half-hour. Hang tight and I'll show you what I found. Bye", I told her as I hung the phone up and made a dash for the door.

As promised, I was back at my office in a few minutes. I wasn't sure at the time but something was telling me this was going to be significant. Much to my surprise, when I walked in Sarah was on the phone. To Lieutenant Akers.

"Hang on Lieutenant, he just walked in", she said as she covered the phone and mouthed to me, "It's Akers. For you."

I took the phone, "Cal?"

"Hey Frank, I've got something a little interesting here on your car."

"Oh?"

"Yeah, it seems that number is a left over, or put to the side, from that '38 series, like I thought."

"And?"

"Well, see, it was never actually issued in the normal sense. It seems it was moved around very quietly in the system and was issued as a covert way of registering the car to the German Foreign Ministry's office in Manhattan."

"Are you kidding me?"

"I double checked it. Even got my nose nipped a little about it."

"Sorry. Do they know it came from me?"

"Not from me but don't be surprised if they do. I mean the guy was already on you."

"Right."

"There's more. It seems this office has direct connections to the Nazi Party's 'Kraft durch Freude' organization."

"Ok Cal, I give up."

"Well Frank, that's the party's wing that uses entertainment and leisure as a means to make their way of life seem attractive. A propaganda tool is all it really is."

"This all sounds good but how's it helping our case?"

"The Deutsche Arbeitsfront, or German Labor Front, another Nazi arm, recently built a fine luxury cruise ship. It's the Robert Ley. It's considered the flag ship of the KdF operation and it's scheduled to arrive in New York day after tomorrow."

"I'm still following all this."

"The guy in your car... following you."

"Yeah?"

"His name is Rudolph Meyer. A member of the German Nazi Party and assigned to the KdF as a diplomatic liaison and he's going to meet the Robert Ley when it arrives. I don't know who he's meeting but it's a good guess they're somebody."

"Maybe another spy?"

"Maybe. The ocean going vessels of the KdF, although completely civilian in appearance and used for civilian luxury cruises are controlled by the Kriegsmarine."

"You mean it's a German Naval vessel?"

"In a manner of speaking, yes."

"So you're thinking this web of intrigue may somehow connect our dead guy and my tail from the other night? This Rudolph Meyer guy?"

"I have no idea Frank. It's all I got right now. You work it out."

I finished with, "Thanks Calvin. Later", and hung the phone up as I started with Sarah. "Are you ready for all this?"

"I'm not sure but go ahead", she said.

"Ok. You better sit down and get ready to take some notes. There's plenty I'm about to throw at ya'."

10

"Alright Sarah, for starters our latest victim was not only arrested for assaulting his wife. It turns out she later died. He killed her."

"Really?"

"I'm serious. You better take some good notes and know how to outline because the waters are about to get real murky here."

"Go ahead Chief, I'm ready."

"Our tail the other day..."

"Yeah?"

"Well he has a name now and he's a German. He's a Rudolph Meyer and he's with the Nazi government. Something to do with the embassy or something. He's here legally and on business."

"How did we find this out?"

"Simple. I matched him to a car and Akers ran the car down. Akers also let me know Meyer is going to meet a German ship here in New York in a couple of days. It's at sea now enroute from Europe."

"Do you think this is all connected back to MaAghon's murder? And the string of previous ones?"

"I have no idea", I told her. And I didn't. All this information had to be linked somehow but right now it was all over the map. "Right now we need to put this down in a way it makes some sort of sense. Make a plan. Let's find out more about that German ship first. Since our tail is going to meet someone getting off I think we should return the favor. I think Akers said it was the Robert Ley. Let's head down to the passenger ship terminal and see what we can learn about this before the Robert Ley gets here."

"So far it's a sound plan. We will need to know the time and which pier it'll dock at to make following Meyer easier."

"Exactly. Let's go", I said as I headed toward the door. Sarah was gathering her things as I took my hat with one hand and reached for the door knob with the other. She was on my heels as we entered the hallway.

The passage from the office to the elevators is usually a dark and drab place. Only a couple of low wattage bulbs in the two spaced apart light fixtures in the high spackled ceiling. The hall is fairly narrow. Almost reminiscent of navigating through a railcar. The walls were of the slat and plaster style with thin tongue-in-groove hardwood slat flooring. There were transom windows above every door along the way. It all added up to cheap rent. Right now that's what I needed too. But for some reason, right at the moment, it felt as though things were about to go our way. The walk down death row to the elevators didn't seem quite so bad today.

We were so low rent we didn't have an elevator operator. It was a do-it-yourself arrangement. When the light indicated the car was there you simply opened a door the same as any other door on the floor. I reached in and pulled the scissoring gate from left to right opening the way into the car. It squeaked and rattled a bit. Sounds like it needs a handy man to lube it or something. I looked back at Sarah, tipped my hat, and gestured for her to enter first. Once in I reached back into the hall and pulled the door shut, grabbed the cage handle and pulled it back across closed, and moved the lever to the right to lower the car down the shaft. Nothing fancy here. It's just a step up from being a freight elevator but it beats walking up and down the stairs.

Once out of the elevator you get a feeling the place isn't that bad. The lobby is well appointed and spacious. The building does house many other tenants and businesses so the owners do tend to make allowances for the higher end clientele. This, of course, helps me out quite a bit. They're not doing anything to make the place better on my account, I can assure you.

"See any German spies scoping us out?" asked Sarah as we walked across the lobby.

"Very funny."

"Well?"

"You'll think funny when they decide we're getting too close to something", I answered. "Plus I really have no idea how much the Feds know and where they're at on this. I don't want to upset their apple cart either."

"Now that part does bother me."

"It should. They can actually do something to us", I said to Sarah as I held the door for her.

We emerged from the relative silence of the lobby interior out into the bright sunlight and blaring sounds of motor traffic and car horns. As we walked the three blocks back down East 57th Street to get my car there was very little conversation. Pedestrian traffic along the sidewalk and the traffic noise pretty much prevented it. It was alright though. We'd be at my apartment building in a few minutes.

About half way along our three block walk I thought I could hear a steady low tone that was just detectable above all the other street noises. It was enough to make me stop walking and tilt my head to one side like Nipper. Of course, Sarah stopped walking too and looked at me like I was purple.

"Are you alright?" she asked.

Without moving or looking at her I asked, "Can't you hear that?" The hum seemed just a bit louder now.

"Hear what?"

Suddenly the hum was monstrous and everyone walking along the street stopped and looked straight up through the buildings.

"That!" I said, as we watched the nose of an airship come into view as it began crossing 57th Street near Park

Avenue. She was moving from our left to our right. More or less in a southerly direction. And just above building height. The engines could be heard over everything else.

"Is that a dirigible?" she asked.

"Not really. After what happened over in New Jersey they pretty much stopped using those. But almost the same thing."

"Then what the heck is that thing?" she continued as the behemoth slowly floated above the street and gradually disappeared over the buildings on our side. The discernible engine sound had returned to a muffled hum as the ship continued southward over the rooftops and out of sight of us standing at the bottom of the steel and concrete canyon.

"The Navy still uses a variation of 'em but they're much safer. I think there may be some civilian uses but they don't carry passengers anymore. My guess is that one is on its way to the Empire State Building on a mail run."

"Too bad about that accident in New Jersey. I thought about one of those trips before that happened."

"Stick to ocean cruises. Much nicer and safer anyway. Like you have a choice."

"Well, why don't you take me to the passenger ships then?"

"You know what? I think I will", I said as we walked up to my parked car. "Get in", I said to her as I opened the driver door and she walked around to the other side.

11

We pulled out of the alley behind my building onto Lexington Avenue and made the quick left to the intersection of East 57th Street. Then left onto East 57th for the straight shot to the Hudson River. We soon crossed the prime meridian of the known universe; 5th Avenue. This is where East 57th became West 57th. And West 57th carried us right up to the waterfront and pier 97. Another three blocks down to West 54th Street and we were there. It was easier going there than driving to the Police Building.

Walking back up 12th Avenue to the new terminal building the big ships could be seen parked in their berths. I asked Sarah, "See those ships parked there?" I pointed to speed up the conversation.

"Yes."

"Do you notice anything a little odd?"

"Not really. No. What?"

"Notice in those last few spaces down there the two parked nearest the last ship", I said.

"I see them."

"They're completely painted over in drab gray. The others are black trimmed in white with red smoke stacks sticking up in the air for the world to see."

"Alright. I still don't follow you."

"It's a sign, albeit subtle to us, there is a major war going on in the rest of the world. Those ships still operate as civilian cruise liners but flagged by countries at war. I've read some newspaper accounts of German U-boats even sinking civilian ships."

"Sinking unarmed cruise ships!?"

"I'm afraid so. Germany sank the British civilian ocean liner Lusitania in the Great War. That pretty much got us into it too."

"Surely nothing would happen here in New York", she reassured herself.

"Probably not. If it were to happen you'd still be alright up here in Manhattan. If anything did happen it would probably be in 'The Narrows' between the Upper and Lower Bays."

"What!?"

"Forget it. The Navy and Coast Guard have it covered like white on rice. It'll never happen. But I really do fear before long we will be involved in this war just as we were last time."

About now we entered the terminal building and began to scope things out. Surprisingly there didn't seem to be that many people around. It certainly didn't hold a candle to the train stations. The layout was quite different as well with the building being so narrow and immensely long. Nothing like anything in the city. But I guess it needed to be to accommodate the great length of these newer and bigger ships. Since we were still in a peacetime posture there were operating terminals for every nation running cruise lines. Even those we were having nervous relations with. Sarah and I split up to read all the boards for arrivals and departures. She along one side and I the other. We would meet back up at the far end.

I managed to reach the rendezvous point first and decided to just wait there rather than work my way back toward her. Anything could have side tracked her and I didn't want to have to waste time hunting her down.

"Frank!" she yelled out to me from out of nowhere. I turned to see her still walking toward me.

"There you are. Ready to go?" I replied.

"Go? What are you talking about? Sit down", she said as she gestured to some nearby benches.

"Alright. Got something?" I asked as I sat.

Easing down next to me Sarah continued with, "Get something? You bet I did."

"Care to share it with me?"

"I'm not sure if I do or not. You're awfully fast to throw in the towel, aren't you?'

"I just figured-"

"You just figured if the great Frank DeGrae didn't find what we're looking for it wasn't here; and the fact I'm a girl. Well buster, you better hat check that crap or I'll start my own private line into the mayor's office. I don't need this."

"Whoa...whoa...whoa with all that. Jiminy Christmas Sarah, take a pill. I'm sorry. Now what did you find."

After a moment of silence accompanied by pursed lips and a stare that could cut diamonds she finally spoke. "Alright Frank. This is what we know now. There is a German liner by the name of Robert Ley scheduled to arrive over on that side at 12:45 tomorrow afternoon. That was posted on the leader board. Simple to get."

"And you got all upset with me because...?"

"Because I also spoke with a steward."

"Okay?"

"Being a girl has its advantages. Getting past a long story I also have a copy of the passenger manifest. We can get a jump on who's aboard tonight."

"Now that's my girl. I'm sorry I ever doubted you. Let's go."

I looked down the terminal hall as we stood and I noticed about fifty yards or so away, walking toward us, were three men all dressed identically. Almost the look of gangsters or G-men. Or maybe from the Nazi attaché.

"Sarah, quick, in here." I grabbed her by the arm and pulled her into a doorway behind me. "I think some fellas from the German embassy may be out there looking for us. There were three very serious looking gentlemen all wearing black suits walking our way."

"German officials? Looking for us?"

"I would venture to say they may even be Staatspolizei."

"Staats-whats?"

"Gestapo. The Gestapo. Heard of them? We've got to get out of here and now."

We had unknowingly entered a boarding passage on my side of the terminal. And lucky for us there was still a liner berthing there. We were onboard a ship and no one knew it but Sarah and me. For the moment. When I finally figured this out I told Sarah and told her to follow me.

"I'm not sure they saw us or know if we're still here. But I'm taking no chances. Let's go."

"Go where?"

"Away from here. Let's go that way. Back toward the street. Maybe we can find another boarding passage we can get out of here down there."

"Fine. Let's go."

We managed to get back on dry land and wasted no time getting out of Hell's Kitchen. Parked near West 42nd Street I just took it straight back to the heart of Manhattan. In no time we made it to Times Square and ran 42nd straight on until we hit Lexington Avenue. Left on Lexington and we were home free.

"That was fun", Sarah said as we cruised along.

"So, anything on your list we should know about?" I asked.

Sarah pulled a folded piece of yellow legal pad paper out of her purse, mumbled a bit, and tossed it on the floor. Before it settled her hand was back in the purse. She was digging around in it like a squirrel digging for a buried nut.

"Don't leave your trash in my car."

"I'll get it."

"Having trouble there?"

"Just drive. I'll take care of this."

Back at the office Sarah and I had finally settled into our respective chairs with coffee and started combing through her list of passengers.

"So Frank, do you always have this much fun with people who may want to make you disappear?"

"Oh this was a walk in the park. Just wait", I said as I shook out a Camel and reached for a match.

"That's what I'm afraid of."

"You came to me, remember? Now let's work on this list."

"Frank?" Sarah said as I lit my smoke.

"What now?"

"You do realize if those guys at the ship terminal were really after us they already know where your office and apartment are."

"Uh... yeah, I guess they do." She actually got me to thinking. I don't know how I could have been so boneheaded as to not have already thought about that. "Let's look at this right now, alright?" I said to her as I picked the list back up off the desk and took a draw from my cigarette.

"You know those things are bad for you, don't you?"

"Everything I do is bad for me. Leave me alone."

12

"How about we cover a little more area? Since you got the passenger list you comb through that. I'm going back down to records and pull the criminal histories of all the victims on our list."

"Sounds ok to me. Are we looking for something in particular?" Sarah replied.

"I'm sure we are. Right now I still don't know what the common denominator is but I know it's there somewhere."

"I agree. But I'm not staying here alone. I'm going back to my place to finish this. After that last little adventure I have a bad feeling about you having some visitors."

"You might ease back into your home turf. If you're right I'm sure they've figured out who you are by now too."

"I can handle myself, thanks."

"I know you can. I'm just saying have a 'Plan B'. You may need to stay somewhere else for a while. I'm working on the same thing so don't get your shorts tangled up."

"What?" Sarah said with one raised eyebrow.

"Look sister, you wanted to be my partner. Before long you're very likely to hear worse than that so lighten up."

"Alright hero, this can work both ways. Now let's cut the crap and get out of here. We have work to do."

I picked up my hat and headed for the door. "You wait a few minutes. I'll leave first alone just in case we have another shadow in the lobby."

"Thanks Frank. Sorry about getting snippy. I just-"

"Never mind. Just wait. I'll get with you later. Be careful."

"You too."

I eased the door open and slowly checked the hallway. It was clear but I really didn't want to strut through the lobby again. I was fairly sure there would be someone waiting for me. Maybe this time more than one. I really didn't want to burn my emergency escape route either so I skipped the elevator all together and went straight to the stairwell at the opposite corner from the one I used last time. You gotta' keep 'em guessin'.

Later that evening when I finally got home I turned on the radio. "At the tone, it's 10 P.M., B-U-L-O-V-A, Bulova watch time. WABC, New York." After a short pause the hum could be heard then came, "Chesterfield brings you the Moonlight Serenade" followed by Glenn Miller starting his show with his hit song. I left the volume up as I walked around the apartment taking my tie off and emptying my pockets of keys and loose change into a dish on the corner of my telephone table. By now I had kicked off my shoes and poured a bourbon. I was walking back to my desk in time to hear Patty, Maxene, and Laverne half-way through Rum and Coca Cola. I guess it had been one of those days for them too. I sat down and reached across to turn the volume down just enough to hear the background noise of the music. I couldn't decide if I should look into these folders or just call it a day and turn in. I was washed out. I was certain if I finished my drink I was finished.

Before I knew it I had glossed over three of the histories and heard Moonlight Serenade strike up again on the radio. "See you next Tuesday at this same time. If you're in New York why don't you drop in and hear Glenn at the Pennsylvania Hotel or at the Paramount Theater where the band and the Andrews Sisters are appearing in person", came the announcer's voice over the music as the program was signing off. I had somehow managed to sit at my desk and read these files for the entire time of the show. And the worst part... my brain was in a fog and I couldn't remember a word I'd seen. I'd had enough. I went to bed.

oOo

It was about 9:00 o'clock in the morning when the phone rang. The ringing grew louder until the bell sounded like the clanging of a school yard bell. I stirred from some pretty sound sleep and was a bit unsettled at first. I was sleeping so hard I was still flummoxed when I sat up trying to find the phone.

Grabbing the receiver I yelled, "What!?" before putting it to my ear or picking up the horn to speak into.

"Frank?"

"What? Who is this?" I shouted while trying to rise and fumble with the lamp. Then I realized the sun was up and I didn't need it.

"Frank, Sarah. Are you gonna' sleep all day? We've got work to do."

"What?"

"What happened? You have a hot date last night or something?"

"I'm up. I'm getting dressed too. Get over to the office. I'm on my way as soon as I can get out of here. I found something that may interest you."

"Oh really. This is our lucky day then. I'll see you in a little while. Bye."

"Lucky day? What do you-?" She hung up before I could finish. I guess I'd find out soon enough. Sitting on the edge of the bed I still had sand in my head and cotton in my mouth. I felt like crap. I leaned forward and hung the receiver back on the candle stick. I kept telling myself I would get a regular phone but then would talk myself out of it. After all it was just for the bedside.

I grabbed my zippo and pack of Camels from next to the phone and started for the kitchen. I was in a hurry but I was having coffee before I did anything. I struck a large kitchen match and lit the front left stove eye. I decided to use that flame to light my smoke and save the flint and naphtha. With my cigarette lit I sat the percolator on the stove. I had the foresight last night to load it before turning in.

Waiting for the pot to boil I strolled back to my desk, still in my slippers and robe, and eased around behind it. Still standing I took a draw from my smoke and flipped open one of the file folders that was lying there from last night. Just as some things seemed to be coming into view I heard the pot come to life. I returned to the kitchen to turn the flame down low to keep from burning the coffee. I stood there focused on the low blue flame like a moth but I was also beginning to see a possible link among our little group of victims. Today could prove to be rather interesting after all.

13

Getting off the elevator I saw Sarah standing at the office door. "I was wondering if you were coming", she said.

"Just hold your horses missy, I've got some hot info for you when we get in there." She produced quite a scowl with pursed lips and one raised eyebrow. But for some reason she appeared to have talked herself out of saying anything. I know this was hard for her but she also wanted to get right to the business at hand too. I unlocked the door and she almost pushed me aside to get in.

"Ok Dick Tracy, what'd'ya have?"

"Well hang on hot pants, where's the fire? I'm gettin' it. Sit down for Pete's sake. Better yet, cool your engines and make some coffee. This is going to take more than a minute. And by the way, what have you got for us?"

"Hang on, I'm making some coffee", she said as she left the room.

I took the opportunity to sit down at my desk and start placing the folders around in a strategic pattern for the presentation when Sarah got back.

Walking back in from the front office Sarah chimes in, "Alright Frank, let's get started", as she set my cup on the corner of the desk and took a seat. She raised her cup for a sip and I began.

"Something in particular has bugged me about this for a while and I think I finally nailed it down."

"Do tell."

"I made the cardinal mistake of thinking the police had looked at all their own stuff. It appears not."

"What are you talking about?"

"All the victims. The Dead Club boys. They all have criminal arrest records. And they're all local. The boys down at the Police Building had all the files right at their fingertips but apparently glossed over some things."

"What've ya' found?" Sarah asked in a genuinely inquisitive tone as she eyed the spread out file folders across the desk.

"I've read all of these until my eyes are crossing and I want you to do the same. Just in case I've missed something too. But I don't think so."

"Alright. What is it, already?"

"They've all been arrested for assaulting a wife or girlfriend-"

"Who hasn't in this town?"

"If I'm allowed to finish... that ended with their victims being outright murdered at the scene or dying later in a hospital."

"Run that by me again", Sarah requested in a much softer tone.

I replied, "That's right Sarah, they all killed their significant other in a domestic spat. Just at the moment I'm not quite sure what this means but it's the first real common link among our victims I've seen. We need to try to run this angle down a little more."

"Agreed. It does have the smell of being significant. Did Akers, or anyone down there, ever mention this?"

"Not this. Akers did tell me about this last guy but never anything about the rest. And he didn't mention the assault victim had died. I'm guessing he didn't bring it up because he didn't know. I know he wouldn't have kept it from me."

Sarah continued with, "Let's pull the details out of those files and condense 'em onto our own flow chart so we can see how they might correlate."

I gathered the folders up and after they were back in a neat stack I handed half to Sarah. "Here. You do these and I'll do the rest." Without saying anything she rose from the chair, took them, and headed for the front office. As she turned her back to me and started for the door she said, "Doughnuts are on the table", without stopping or looking back.

After taking a sip from my cup I said, "Thanks." I picked up the first folder from my pile and thought here comes the fun part of the job.

Although we got a late start when early evening came it felt like we'd been at it for days. I was so taxed my brain felt like it was in a fog and it was done for the day.

"Frank", said Sarah as she walked in carrying her whole library. I looked up and she followed on with, "I'm done."

"What?"

"Let's call it a day. Hungry?"

I put my last folder down and answered, "As a matter of fact I was thinking the same thing. Let's get out of here."

"I'm game. Let's go", she said.

Without another word we each gathered our things and headed for the door. Neither of us even mentioned where to go. We just went. I'm sure she felt no different than I did and just needed a break.

When we stepped off the elevator I said, "Here's a café right off the lobby. Let's just step in there and forget about trying to go somewhere."

"Sounds fine to me."

I figured somebody had camped out in the lobby waiting for us but right now I really couldn't care any less about that. He could pull up a chair if he wanted. I stepped just ahead of Sarah as we approached the glass and chrome door to the coffee shop and pulled it open. Sarah moved past me and through the door. I looked back across the lobby behind us and then made my entrance behind her. I saw no one in the lobby. I guess if someone was there he punches a clock. That proves it. He was a government employee.

oOo

Sarah had just hung her coat on one of the chrome coat hooks near the door as I took off my hat. I placed it on the shelf above her coat and followed her once again. The shop was also empty but wasn't supposed to close for at least another hour so we found a booth near the front window and settled in. It was beginning to get dark out but the traffic outside looked as heavy as it ever does. Everyone in the city had to be somewhere other than where they were.

"What'l'ya'have?" asked the waitress. We both snapped our heads around from staring out the window to see a woman of about thirty years with her hair pulled back and one of those little nurse looking cap things pinned to the top of her head. No makeup and a uniform with a few stains here and there. She looked like she's been here for two days.

"Has it been a long day?" I asked with a slight smile. I was hoping to garner a smile in return along with some good service.

"Oh brother, what a day it's been. Help calling off and me having to pull a double. But that's alright. I can use the money. Now hun, what can I get ya'?" she finished with a smile and an upbeat tone at the end. I think I made headway.

"Sarah, know what you want?" I asked.

"I'll just have a Club sandwich and Coke", she said without looking up from the menu.

I never picked one up but followed up with, "Just a BLT and I'll have a Coke too. Thanks."

The waitress finished scribbling on her pad, looked over it down at me, smiled and said, "I'll get that right out to you sweetie", and spun around for the kitchen.

Sarah folded the menu closed and placed it in its holder. When she looked across the table at me I told her, "Darlene should be back any minute with our Cokes."

"You know her?"

"No."

"Really? Then how–"

"You must be tired. Ever heard of nametags?" There came that glare again. "So what do you make of things so far?"

Sarah's face morphed back to her normal attractive self and almost mustered a smile when she replied, "I think I see a definite pattern but I don't get where Nazis come into it."

"What do you mean?"

"Well what I'm seeing is the possibility of someone playing 'Angel of Death' for the benefit of these murdered women. Although it is early and some of that could be my imagination at work."

"Could be. I'm beginning to see the benefit of a woman's point of view on some of these things. I'm so focused on this Nazi thing you could be right. I mean, we know McAghon was tangled up with those guys. He had an apartment no one in his line of work could afford and some of his Nazi buddies are now following us around."

"And?" she said.

"I don't know. Right now I still just don't know. Let's follow up on any theory right now. We can't let anything fall through the cracks."

"Agreed. For now how about I take all these criminal history files and dig deeper in that direction and you go back to looking at your Nazi friends."

"Sounds good. It's time we cover more ground a little quicker. You do that and get 'em back to Akers while I head back to 'The Pit'."

"'The Pit'?"

"Yeah. The other day when I was down there Tommy told me about some mysterious woman coming by asking about McAghon but she wouldn't tell anyone down there who she was."

"Alright then. Sounds promising."

"When they asked for information to update her she just told 'em she'd come back."

"Sounds very interesting."

Darlene showed up with a large tray carrying everything. I was wrong once again. She hadn't brought the Cokes out ahead of time. Without a word she quickly placed our plates and little green six-ounce glasses in front of us, then flatware rolled up in napkins, followed by straws. "Do you need anything else, hun?" she asked.

"No, thanks Darlene. It looks fine", I answered.

"Alright then. Just let me know if I can get you anything else."

"Thanks. I will", I said as she turned away.

Sarah commented, "I'm sure glad I'm with you."

"Oh?"

"Yeah. Your friend Darlene hasn't even looked in my direction much less spoke to me."

"Jealous?"

"No. Just hungry thank you very much. Go ahead and saddle up to that if you like. I couldn't care less."

"Riigghhtt..." I slowly said as I picked up the first half of my sandwich. "You're a fast mover there. You've got me going from a BLT to out on a date in fifteen minutes. Can we get back to the case now?"

"I never left it Mr. 'size 10 hat'."

"What does that mean?"

"Nothing. Forget it. Let's get back to business here."

"Good", I said as I finally got to take a bite. We were both hungrier than we thought. When we started to eat the conversation stopped.

14

Stirring awake I noticed the slightest hint of a coming sunrise through the closed blinds. Then again it could have just been a nearby streetlight. It was still dark out but not for long. I looked at the clock. 5:08 A.M. and the ticking came to my attention. It was the only thing I could hear. I threw back the blanket and sat up on the side of the bed. I picked up the clock and looked at it once more. 5:10. I wound the key on the back and set it back on the table. 5:11.

I stood and walked toward the dresser next to the bathroom door. It seemed to be a shade lighter outside. I turned on the radio and picked up the half empty pack of Camels as it warmed up. Striking a match, I lit my smoke as the broadcast gradually grew loud enough to hear. Taking the first draw I could tell it was becoming morning out. The light from outside was much more pronounced as it found its way in between the slats of the rolled down blinds. I walked over and pulled the string to cant the louvres and brightened up the room. I was tempted to close them back.

Checking the dial I was searching for the clearest Columbia Broadcasting station in hopes of finding another Elmer Davis update on the war. So far it seemed the Nazis were a powerhouse in Europe. Before long they'd be controlling everything over there. They had recently launched their Saar Offensive and were now knocking on Paris' front door.

Although Fritz Kuhn had finally been sent to prison the American Nazis and Hitler sympathizers were still operating in the open and having rallies only now led by Gerhard Kunze and with much smaller crowds. With things heating up like they are this can't go on much longer. Germany is at war with virtually every allied nation. Try as we may to stay out of this thing I don't see it.

It was about 9:00 A.M. when I got to the morgue. I walked in through the back service entrance and immediately saw Anne sitting at her station. When the door opened she quickly turned and looked in my direction as well.

"Well if it isn't Frank DeGrae again", she said in an almost sarcastic tone.

"Good morning, Anne. Any news about McAghon or his mystery visitor?"

"I don't know anything about him but that woman did come back. We have some contact information about her now."

"You do?"

"It may be fake but we told her we had to have it before we could release any information."

"Well, it's something."

"Hang on while I get it", she said as she pushed back from the desk and rose from her chair. She turned and opened a nearby filing cabinet.

"Here. Here it is", Anne said as she pulled out a large index card and handed it to me.

Taking it, I said, "Thanks" and looked it over.

"Go ahead and write it down. I don't care. I never saw you."

I sat it on the corner of the desk and took out my notepad and pen. "Thanks darlin'. You're a sweetheart", I said while jotting down my notes. "Is Milano around?" I asked while still bent over scribbling.

"Yeah, he's still in his office. He hasn't gone to work yet."

"Thanks", I replied as I looked up from the desk, placed my notebook in my jacket pocket, and turned for the door leading to the suite of offices toward the front of the building. I got here early enough today I didn't have to navigate through the labyrinth of 'The Pit' again.

Entering the adjacent hallway I called out, "Tommy?"

"I'm in here", came an answer from farther down the hall. I walked on down to the small interior office Milano uses.

As I turned into his doorway he looked up. "So what brings you down here?"

"I just came down to check on our guy McAghon again. I wanted to ask a favor too."

"Shoot."

"The murder weapon? They were scissors, weren't they?"

"They were."

"Were the others the same?"

"As a matter of fact they were. Exactly the same. We still have them all down here. No one downtown has picked 'em up yet. I guess since no one has been arrested or getting ready for trial they figured the evidence could stay down here."

"No prints?"

"Somebody came down here to process that and they all showed clean."

"I see. I shouldn't be surprised. Anything else you can tell me about them?"

Milano stood and walked around the desk. "Come with me" he said as he brushed past me and out the door. I followed. At a brisk pace he continued talking as I followed.

"You can see for yourself what these things look like. And while you're at it I'll give you the breakdown."

"Thanks."

We entered another room just down the hall off of the main hallway of the exam rooms. It was much larger than most rooms in the building. It housed cabinets mounted to the wall, free standing cabinets, filing cabinets, shelves with various body parts and fluids in specimen jars of varying sizes, refrigerators, lock boxes, and on and on. Everything appeared to be labeled or tagged in some configuration to catalogue everything but it was all Latin to me. I followed Tommy down an aisle that brought us to a large free standing cabinet in what I was guessing to be about the center of the maze. Standing in the middle of a long narrow aisle it was most difficult to gauge where we really were. I found myself standing in what was essentially a very large and creepy warehouse.

"Here", he said as he stopped and opened the right side of the double doors. He pulled out a deep drawer containing several large Manila envelopes. "These are the addendums to the files of the 'scissor' victims along with the scissors removed from each one at autopsy."

"How nice."

"Hey, somebody's got to do this."

"I know. Where can I actually get these thing out and look at them?"

Milano reached in and gathered them all up into one large bundle and while holding them all to his chest with both arms said, "Follow me." We were off again toward the other end.

At a nearby table he set them all down and started opening the packages. One by one he reached in and removed a blood stained pair of large scissors. Each had its own paper tag attached by a thin tan-colored string to one of the handle rings. The scissors all looked identical. The only way to distinguish them from one another would be by their tags. All five pair were now lying side by side in a neat row.

"So this is the infamous collection of scissors?" I asked.

"It is indeed, Frank. These are actually known as the J. Wiss & Sons Pinking Shears model 'A'. They only had two different models and the difference is really only in their length."

"I see."

"These, like I said, are the 'A' model scissors, being the larger of 'em. They are ten and a half inches long whereas the smaller pair are nine inches. Not really a lot of difference."

"Especially when it comes to getting stabbed through the heart", I added.

"I would agree", he said as he picked one up and operated it opening and closing the blades.

"What's with those teeth?" I said. When the blades opened I could see these incredible saw teeth on the blades' edges. These things looked like murder weapons.

"These are sewing scissors. Also called pinking scissors. Or pinking shears. They're designed for cutting fabric in a certain way. They were actually designed and invented here in New York about ten years ago."

"Interesting."

"These all appear to be identical. Possibly bought by the same person all at the same time. Each is marked by the manufacturer, each is of the model 'A' length of ten and a half inches, and each has the black enameled finger rings. I have no doubt these were acquired and used by the same person. Unofficially Frank, I would say you are dealing with a serial killer here."

"I think so too Tommy. The odds of these murders done in this fashion pretty much rule out being done by different people and completely unconnected. Even the style in which they're used nails it down."

"Let me know if I can be of any more help."

"Thanks Tommy. I need to run now. I'll see ya' later", I said as I started out.

15

I decided I would first run back down to the Police Building and see Akers. I would get up with Sarah later but for now I wanted to try to ID our mystery lady who was McAghon's friend. We may have a pretty good lead here and I couldn't let it run cold. I thought I would call before making the trip but once outside I couldn't see a phone. Then I remembered there were a couple of payphones back inside in the main front lobby.

Walking back in, Anne looked up and when she saw me there was a bewildered look on her face. Before she could ask, I volunteered, "I'm heading up front to use a phone." Her opened mouth went back closed and she returned to whatever it was she was doing.

When I emerged from the hall into the lobby I dug into my pocket for some loose change. I picked out a buffalo nickel as I got to the first booth and dumped the other change back into my pocket. They changed up the nickel a couple of years ago but there were plenty of the old ones still floating around. The door of the oak booth was already open so I simply sat down and picked up the receiver. I dropped the coin into the slot at the top right of the phone and pulled the door shut. I heard the clickety-click of the dropping coin and then the dial tone. We were in business.

"Lieutenant Akers, may I help you?" answered Calvin

"Cal. Frank. You busy?"

"Frank. Good to finally hear from you. Anything going on?"

"I can be down there in just a few. I'm leaving 'The Pit' right now. See you in a minute", I said and hung the phone up.

A short time later I was parking behind the Police Building. Having just spoken to Calvin I didn't bother to stop at any receptionists' stations and went straight up to his office. I also didn't hang around the lobby waiting for an elevator either. Calvin was just on the second floor so I took the main stairs.

Walking into Akers' office unannounced seemed to be a bit of a surprise to him. Stepping in as I did, he quickly diverted his attention from his desk top to the door. He almost looked as if he'd been hit by a little jolt. He did however quickly recover.

"What the-"

"Be nice now. Got a minute?"

"I have lots of minutes. What's up?"

Just as I was about to sit down the phone rang. Akers picked it up. "Lieutenant Akers, may I-." After a short silent pause he continued with, "What? Wait a minute. Who is this?" He sat quiet. Presumably listening to whoever was on the other end again. After about a minute he hung the phone up without saying another word and rose from his chair.

"You can come along if you like", he said to me as he stepped from behind the desk.

"Where're we headed?" I said as I followed him back to the door.

"There's a guy in an alley trash bin about a half a block from the Passenger Ship piers at 45nd street. Throat cut. Let's go", Akers said while never stopping. He was putting on his coat, hat, and walking around all the while.

"We were just down around there not long ago. I'll fill you in on the ride over", I told him.

The scene was just less than fresh. When we pulled up the alley had already been closed off at each end with patrol cars. Uniforms were standing behind Al's Barber

Shop just off the street in the alley. Akers stopped his car next to the parked patrol unit and shut it down.

Both car doors closing in tandem I paused giving Akers time to walk around to my side. As we started for the curb I just had to throw out, "So I don't guess you're worried about double parking?" He just cut his eyes at me and we kept walking.

"So where's our guy?" Akers addressed the uniforms. They turned slightly with one of them raising his arm pointing further back into the alley.

"Back there Lieutenant. I think Gerard's down there. We haven't been back there. Just blocking the alley."

Akers started forward and I fell in line. We passed between the two officers and started for a pile of wooden barrels stacked behind a printer's warehouse. Most of the buildings were of old red clay brick construction with one exception. Just about mid-block there was still one old three-story wooden building holding out against progress. I wasn't sure of what was in there. We never walked that far down. The whole area generally had that waterfront industrial feel about it.

Nearing the barrels and two more of New York's finest, Akers again asked, "So what's up boys?"

Pointing to one particular barrel only feet away we hear from one, "He's in there Lieutenant."

Akers and I eased closer to one of the larger fifty-five gallon barrels. The top had already been removed and was lying on the cobbled brick alley a couple of feet away.

"One of the guys came out to get another one and found this guy", said the officer. "He's sitting over there waiting to talk to you."

"Thanks", said Akers as he stared into the barrel.

"Well it's a safe bet he didn't work down here", I said.

"Do ya' think?" came Akers.

"Hey, look here", I said pointing down into the barrel at his neck. "His neck wasn't just cut. Someone garrotted him. Look closer. The wire is still there."

Bending over to take a closer look Akers replied, "I think you're right. Yes I see it now. It took a minute since it's such a bloody mess in there."

Milano's Pit crew arrived and we casually moved out of their way to extract our customer from the barrel. "Let me know before you guys leave", Akers told them and then we walked over to the witness.

"Lieutenant!" we heard from the barrel crew. Akers quickly turned to look. "Hold on." He turned back to the workman and said, "That'll be enough for now. Somebody may be getting back to you. Thanks", and we headed back.

Once the guy was laid out flat on a gurney he did look quite different. I said, "He looks familiar."

Akers turned to me, "He does?"

"I think that's the guy who you got the tag and ID for me. My shadow from the office lobby back to my apartment."

As I continued talking one of the attendants handed Akers a wallet. He opened the wallet and I kept talking. After a moment Akers interrupted with, "I think you're right Frank. This stuff does say he's the KdF guy Rudolph Meyer."

"What the... what's going on here?"

"I'm not sure but it looks like you better find out."

The morgue guys started to roll him out calling back, "Lieutenant, need anything else?"

I called out, "Wait!" and started for the gurney. They stopped and looked at me. I followed up with, "Do you guys still have the wire?" They looked across the gurney at each other. "The murder weapon? That thing stuck in his neck?" I continued.

"Oh, yeah. It's still there. We haven't moved it."

I walked over and Akers followed. "What are you thinking?" he asked.

"Not sure yet. Just looking", I answered.

Akers and I both leaned in a little closer and examined the actual laceration to the throat and the garrotte used to do the deed still in place.

I took my pen from my jacket pocket and lifted the handle of one side then walked around and lifted the other slightly. "This looks like a rather hasty last minute kind of thing", I said while still looking down.

"Do tell", Akers replied in a rather sarcastic tone.

Standing back from my leaning posture I turned to him and said, "For starters the handles are not of metal. They're wood. Hastily made from sawing off short sections of a broom or mop handle. Notice they're painted but the cut ends are bare wood. One handle even has one rounded finished end that wasn't cut. The very end of the original handle."

"Oh... yeah, I think you may be right."

"And the wire was also an item of convenience. It is a repurposed 'E' string from a violin."

"Oh come on now. That is a bit thin."

"Precisely. Very thin. Look here", I said as I pointed to the handle on our guy's left side. "Here where the wire is pushed through the tiny hole of the stick you'll see the ball, the little piece of round metal that looks more like a tiny wheel that the wire is wound on."

"Ok. Yeah I see it", Akers said.

"Look over there and you won't see any of this. Just the wire tied off in a rudimentary fashion."

"Oh yeah, I do see what you're talking about. Go ahead."

"Violin strings, rather than say, a guitar, also have the strings color-coded on this end too. Guitar strings do not. Other instruments larger than a violin would be ruled out since their strings are thicker. You want one as thin as possible for this job."

"Alright. I'm still listening."

"The length of the string looks about right for a violin as well as a garrotte. No one would take the time to shorten up a long guitar string and this one also still has the little bridge bumper. No guitar strings have those. And again, notice the color at the part that is wound around the ball."

"So, you're saying this is an improvised homemade weapon made from a violin string and broom stick?"

"A violin 'E' string and the cut ends of a broom stick. Or mop handle", I answered. "The 'E' string is also the thinnest of the violin strings."

"So the killer is a violin player?" asked Akers.

"Yes. Or someone who works on violins. Or sells musical instruments and accessories. Or someone who found a discarded string. I don't know Calvin. Do I have to figure everything out for you?"

"Funny Frank. Very funny."

"I can say I do believe this is probably connected in some bizarre way to this same stuff I'm on. This is the guy who followed me. But you have a different killer too. This is not the work of the McAghon killer. And who knows, maybe for an entirely different reason than what we're focused on. It may be some cloak and dagger stuff."

"Could be. I need to get with Ellison on this. We may be able to just hand this off to his office and keep focusing on our scissors killer."

"Sounds solid to me."

"Alright guys, you can have him", Akers told the 'Pit' boys. We all started walking for the exit of the alley and back to the street. Just as we made it to the sidewalk we met one of my dearest former colleagues, Detective Randall Van Wort."

"Well, hello gentlemen", he said, stopping just short of walking into us. After a quick double take he followed up with "Well... if it isn't Frank DeGrae. What are you doing on this scene?" with his usual condescending tone and a special emphasis on 'you'.

"Oh, I don't know Randy. Maybe they wanted the help of a real detective on this one."

"Very funny Frank. You might want to clear off my scene."

Akers kicked in with, "You might want to go on and play with your jacks and back off. Frank is here with me and is working with us with approval of the Mayor's office.

If you have a problem with seeing him out here take it up with the Chief's office."

"Oh, ignore him Randy. We were just leaving anyway. See you in the funny papers pal", I said.

"Kiss off Frank", answered Van Wort.

As we walked down the street to Akers' car and the morgue crew loaded Rudy Meyer in the wagon Calvin had to ask, "So what's the deal with you two? You guys have been at each other as far back as I can remember."

"You'll have to ask Marion about that."

"McKinley? Marion McKinley? Is that behind that 'Ice Princess' act she put on at McAghon's apartment?"

"Could be."

16

I made it back to my office late in the day. In fact, by the time I made it upstairs it was dark. Fumbling for my keys as I stepped off the elevator I looked up in time to see Sarah come out into the hall.

We both stopped in our tracks as we looked at one another and I said, "Well hello stranger. What's new?"

"Plenty. I was hoping you were here so I dropped in. I guess we'll go back in."

"I guess we will", I said as I unlocked the door.

As we entered the back office and I hung my hat up I said, "Alright. Give" and continued on across the room to my desk.

"Ok. You better put on your best listening cap. Do you remember Marius McKinley?"

"You mean the lawyer? Marion's dad?"

"That's the one. And Mark Spencer?"

"Sure I remember Mark. Marius brought him from the public arena into Cromwell and Stirling. And a big pay raise with it."

"And he left Cromwell and Stirling and went back to the D.A.'s office after about a year."

"I remember. And about six months later he was killed in that hotel in Pennsylvania somewhere", I said.

"That's right. Well, actually in New Jersey. A little town called Berlin to the southeast of Philadelphia. Not to be confused with Berlin, Pennsylvania which is near Pittsburgh."

"You have done your homework, haven't you?" I said.

"At the time Spencer was killed there were two women who worked with him on a daily basis in the D.A.'s office. Your friend Marion McKinley and another young lady named Bonnie Waters. You know Marion's story already. She had a lot of help from daddy but Miss Waters was just starting out clerking."

"Wait a minute", I said. "I remember that night at McAghon's apartment when Marion showed up right behind me. She was dressed to the nines and when I commented on it she told me she was the 'on-call' for the prosecutor's office. Pretty snippy about it too."

"I've heard there may be other reasons she gets snippy with you too", said Sarah.

"I say, you really have been doing your homework."

"Yes I have. Now listen."

"No, wait. Listen. She came in and did a walk through with Akers and I stayed away from her. I stood around in the parlor while they went back to the bedroom and checked out McAghon. When they came back up she popped off something rude and headed for the door. On the way she took an ever so slight detour and picked up a small clutch purse that was lying on the end of the couch."

"So?"

"It was the middle of the night and I wasn't really awake at the time but it just came back to me. She didn't walk in carrying anything."

"You mean... she came back? She came to get a handbag she left behind?"

"I'm sure of it now. Yes."

"Could be", Sarah said. "I noticed in the investigator's file on the Spencer murder in New Jersey the hotel manager gave a description of a pretty fancy car parked next to Spencer's in front of his room. Somehow they ran it down as a '38 model BMW 328. The registered owner was an older gentleman who was a golfing buddy with Marion's dad, Marius. Now it's a pretty safe bet that the old guy didn't go out and meet Spencer in a hotel room to kill him but someone else could have borrowed the car."

"Could have but you'll hoe a tough row putting Marion in that car and making it stick."

"I know. A very delicate situation, indeed", Sarah conceded. "Not to mention your 'purse on the couch' story being pretty thin too."

"I know. But it's something. And all we have right now too."

"Maybe. Let's not get back into putting blinders on again either."

"What do you mean?" I asked.

"There is always the other girl to check out too."

"Alright. Let's keep digging on what we do know and we can start running down some of this other girl's background too. But it sure seems to start shaping up that we finally have a suspect with a face and name."

"Now if we can connect her to some Nazis we've hit the jackpot."

"Oh, Sarah, have you heard?"

"Heard what?"

"Our tail. The German guy who kept trying to follow us all the time?"

"He followed you all the time. Nobody ever followed me around town."

"Whatever. Anyway, he was found stuffed in a wooden barrel with a piece of wire almost through his neck down near the passenger ship piers."

"That's a little concerning. Thanks for finally telling me."

"Whoever did it left us a little clue too. It looks like the murder weapon is a homemade garrotte made of short cut pieces of a broom stick and a violin string."

"I give up. Violin string?"

So here I was having to go over the whole, 'this is why it's a violin string' thing again. Sarah was doing so well in the direction she had gone in we decided to keep things as they were. Then suddenly I had an epiphany.

"Hold on a minute", I said as I bolted from my chair and ran to get my jacket. I rifled through the pockets until

I found the hen scratched note I made from Anne's notecard. "What did you say that other girl's name is?"

"Hold on", Sarah said as she started looking through a folder. "Waters. A Bonnie Waters. Why?"

"That mysterious woman who kept visiting the morgue checking up on McAghon finally ID'd herself to Anne as Sibone Walters."

"That's most curious. You may have stumbled onto something Frank. 'Bonnie' is commonly used for 'Sibone'. And of course it's obviously more than a coincidence that one is 'Walters' and the other is 'Waters'."

"Ok... let's say it is the same person. Let's regroup and follow up on each of our two girls. Since I may be biased concerning Marion you take the McKinley file and run it down. And remember, she is still an active assistant prosecutor so be very cautious. I'll keep as far away from that as I can so she doesn't scream it's a personal thing and check out Waters. Or Walters, or whatever her name is."

"Ok Frank", Sarah said as she stood from her chair. "Here is all I have on Waters right now", she said as she handed me one of the many file folders lying around the room. "Double check behind me that I haven't missed any of the McKinley stuff. I don't know her like you do and I need the paperwork."

After a while I figured it was time to call it a day. I started down the sidewalk, stopped and grabbed my obligatory Nathan's, and headed home bumping shoulders with the rest of the world as I tried to eat. Nobody seemed to care I was trying to eat my evening meal. I thought I would start the morning with Waters' personnel file and general stuff first. I figured Sarah was doing the same with Marion. Still, that clutch purse and BMW two-seater at the hotel bothered me. I needed to let that go for now. Sarah was on it.

Morning came but with the pleasant surprise of no one calling during the night. If they did I slept through it. That's ok too. When I sat up I reached for a smoke but they weren't there. I did fall asleep tired. Not only were they not next to the alarm clock, I had no idea where I put 'em. I figured they'd show up somewhere so I went to the kitchen to start the water boiling. I desperately needed coffee.

I headed back to the bedroom to start my morning routine and spotted my suit jacket draped on the back of an accent chair. That seemed odd since I never do that so I walked over and picked it up. While I had it in my hand I checked the pockets and there were the Camels and Zippo in the inside right pocket. I took it as a sign. Today was going to be a good day.

Around nine o'clock I phoned Akers to pick his brain about this Waters girl. Who knows, he may know something about her on his own. She does work down at the D.A.'s office.

"So Calvin... you wouldn't happen to know anything about a girl working down at the D.A.'s office by the name of Bonnie Waters do you?" I asked him.

"Can't say I do. I can't even place her."

After a short conversation we decided I would swing by his office and continue the discussion in person. It was also a little more secure and private too.

"She's young and I think she's just a clerk or something for 'em. I don't think she's a lawyer."

"Probably why I don't know her. I mean, they've got an army of those in there and they come and go like the seasons."

"I figured. Just thought I'd ask."

"So what's her story? Why are you checking her out? Personal or professional?"

"Funny. I don't have a personal life. Not now with this pile of crap you've gotten me mixed up in."

"So you think she may be connected with the case?"

"I don't know. This is just a preliminary thing right now. Probably nothing. Just another loose end I have to tie up. Sarah's doing the same thing with somebody else." I wasn't about to tell him it was Marion McKinley. At least not yet. "So what's the story with Mr. Pickle Barrel?"

"I'm not sure. We handed that thing off to the Feds as quick as we could. From what I can tell it is a cloak and dagger thing. They think his own people did this because he got sloppy and you burned him."

"Well, what do you know? I hate I got him killed. Sorry."

"Not to worry. They'll put a better man on you next time."

"That's what worries me. I think some of 'em tried to hem us up at the piers the other day before he turned up in the barrel."

"If you're not careful it may be one of you in the barrel next", Calvin said.

"Well, we were in the right place for it the other day. We were only about a block from where he was found."

"I know. And the worst part is, if those German government guys invite you to a necktie party there won't be a lot we can do about it. One of 'em could hit you and then catch the next boat or plane out of here. The end."

"That's a nice thought."

"Watch your back. You and Sarah both."

"I'll tell her."

I left Akers' office and walked up the stairs to the top floor. Waters' personnel file should be up there since those aids in the prosecutor's office are also on the city payroll. I could tell I should be taking the stairs more often. I guess I'm getting older.

I got to the window and a new girl I didn't know hopped right over to me asking, "Yes sir? How may I help you?" I was hoping this wasn't going to turn into a roadblock.

"Uh... yes... would you know if Miss Joyner is in today?"

"I'm sorry sir, no she isn't."

"Ok, look, my name is Frank DeGrae and she is-"

"Oh, Mr. DeGrae. It's a pleasure to meet you. I've heard so much about you. I'm Dolly."

She put out her hand and I took it. "Well, Dolly, the pleasure's all mine", I said while shaking it. "Are you new here?" I asked, already knowing she was.

"Yes sir. I've been here five weeks."

I leaned in across the counter that had been affixed to the bottom half of a Dutch door. When the top half was opened it was more commonly known as 'the window'. When I did I also lowered my voice which in turn made Miss Dolly lean closer to me as well. "Listen Dolly, I'm working on something with Lieutenant Akers downstairs and it's imperative anything you and I discuss here be kept in the strictest confidence. I mean, not a word. Alright?"

"Oh, yes sir, absolutely. What do you need from me?"

"Alright. I need you to get me the personnel file on a young lady by the name of Bonnie Waters. She works over in the prosecutor's office. And anything else you may have on file for her up here. And remember, not a word to anyone around here about this."

"Oh, yes sir", she said and quickly disappeared in the maze of barrister cabinets.

So while Dolly was running down my files I was busy doing nothing but hanging out at the window hoping to get things moving along but what should I hear but, "Well hello Frank. What brings you up here to see us?" came another female voice from the inner sanctum. I quickly looked around to see where it came from.

Seeing her blond hair and wide smile I replied, "Well hello Dee. Nice to see you."

"Is it? Then why don't you drop by more often?"

"Here Mr. DeGrae", Dolly said as she approached with a spring in her step and extending to me two tan legal length file folders.

"So what's up Frank?" asked Dee.

"Oh nothing. I'm just grabbing something for Akers. Gotta' run now", and I quickly made my escape. I could hear Dolly and Dee talking as I moved down the hall but I couldn't make out the conversation. I didn't want to. I was just trying to get out of the building.

Walking to the car I quickly scanned the contents of the folders and without reading anything I noticed a four by four glossy snapshot of her stapled to the inside of the second folder. With this piece of gold in hand I was making 'the Pit' my next stop.

After fighting through the usual twenty minutes of traffic between the Police Building and the morgue over by the East River I ran in the service entrance and found Anne at her normal duty station. She was on the phone but turned and looked in my direction with one finger raised in the air indicating I should just stand there and keep my mouth shut. She kept talking.

"Alright then. Thank you... yes... yes... thank you again. Have a great day. Bye."

Anne hung the phone up and turned back to me. "My, my, this is becoming a regular haunt for you isn't it?"

"Do you know this girl?" I ask as I turned the opened folder around to show her the photo.

"Well hello Anne. Nice to see you again Anne", she said without looking at the folder.

"I'm sorry Anne. I'm just in a hurry and forgot all about my manners. I just thought you may have seen this young lady come through here."

Silently she averted her stare down to the folder. After a moment she said, "Wait a minute" and leaned down a little closer. She reached and took the folder from my hand and pulled it even closer to her face as she sat back up. "Yes."

"Yes? Yes what?"

"This is that girl who came in here two or three times and didn't want to tell us who she was." Looking back up at me she continued. "That's the one I gave you on the notecard the other day. Something Walters."

"You're a sweetheart Anne", I said as I reached and took the folder. "Sorry, but I gotta' run. Bye doll", and I turned for the door.

"Bye Frank. Anytime", I heard as I was stepping out into the hall.

I was quick stepping back to the car. I had to get with Sarah but wasn't exactly sure how to go about it right now. I only had one phone number for her and with my luck she would be out pounding the pavement. Since the odds were against me for the moment I figured I'd head back to the office and come up with a new plan then. It would give me a chance to really go through these files too.

Akers got me to thinking about the Meyers guy so I started to develop a small case of paranoia. Once outside I took my time walking down to the car and tried to take everything in. Being in the back lot near the river should have made things easier but I never even considered a sniper. Not until... Next came the crack of a high powered rifle off in the distance but close enough to clearly tell what it was. It was my lucky day, once again, when I also saw one of the two rampant lion statues that stood sentry on either side of the entrance explode. At the angle and height it stood over my left shoulder I couldn't tell how it missed me. But it did and I hit the deck. I quickly got to my knees and fell and stumbled my way back inside. I never heard a second shot ring out. Whoever it was is a one shot Charlie. A professional in that he didn't hang around. Maybe when I proned out he thought he hit me and packed it in then. With that thought I just had an idea.

Lying in the floor just inside the door I heard from down the hall, "What the heck's going on Frank!?"

"Call Akers. Now Anne! Call him. Someone took a shot at me."

"Are you ok!? You hurt?"

"No. I'm fine. They missed. Call Akers and get him down here now!"

I crawled further back into the building until I was well away from the door. I don't think I stood back up until I got to Anne's door. I stepped into her little office space and as I closed the door I could hear her speaking into the phone. She stopped and covered it with her free hand and spoke over it to me. "I've got him on the line now. Want to talk to him?"

"Here", I said as I reached out for it. She turned to me and I took the phone. "Calvin?"

"Frank? You ok? Anne just told me what happened."

"I'm fine but there's one dead lion out back."

"What?"

"Never mind. Look you've got to get down here quick. I've got an idea I need to run by you and I need to do it right now. And I can't leave this building."

"Alright Frank. I'm on the way", and next came the click. I handed the phone back to Anne and stepped back out into the hallway. I reached into my inside jacket pocket, pulled out a half empty pack of Camels, and shook one out. Sliding the pack back where it was I started pacing the hall while I tamped down the smoke on the back of my left hand. Then another idea hit me like a bolt. I stopped walking and tamping. I ran up to the front lobby and to a phone booth.

Pulling the door shut while on the phone I said, "Operator, I need Gramercy 7-7293."

"One moment pu-leeze."

All I could hear inside the seemingly sound proof booth was the ticking of my Timex and the oscillating tone coming over the phone. The ringing of the line seemed to go on forever.

"Hello."

"Sarah? Is that you?" I asked.

"I hope so. I live here and this is my phone."

"Very funny. Look, I'm at the morgue and Akers is on his way down here. Right now I'm stuck here. I need you to get down here too. Quick."

"What's going on?" she asked.

"I can't go into it on the phone. Just get down here."

"Alright Frank. I'm on my way."

"Thanks Sarah. I'll give you the whole story when you get here."

"Ok, bye."

I toggled the hook and the dial tone came back up. I toggled it a few more times and the line went flat and the operator came back on. "Operator, how may I direct your call?"

"Yes ma'am, could you connect me to Spring 7-3200 please?"

"One moment, please", she said and there was silence. Then a click and the low pitched, two on four off, ringback tone came again. I sat waiting.

"Police Department, what's the nature of your call?"

"Yes, this is Frank DeGrae. Could you tell me if Lieutenant Akers is still in his office?"

"He just left the building sir. Could someone else help you?"

"No thanks. I'll see him in a bit", I said as I hung up the phone and took out my gun. I just sat in the booth for a while holding it in my hand just in case someone decided to come in the building and try to finish the job.

17

"So let me get this right. You want me to release to the media that you were killed out here today?" asked Akers.

"Right. See, I think the shooter thought he got me and even if he was guessing, I crawled into the morgue. Surely he saw that if he was hanging around."

"Oh, I get it. Good cover there. But what's the end game?"

"Don't you get it Lieutenant?" Sarah chimed in. "We need to find who these guys are that keep tailing, and now shooting at, Frank. And probably me next. This should give us a little breathing room."

"Right. If they think they got me they'll stop. Then we can come up on their flank", I added.

"Ok Frank. We'll give it a try. But you watch your back anyway. You never know."

"Thanks Calvin. Let's get this game rolling then", I said as we all got up from the little conference table in the staff meeting room.

"I almost forgot", I said.

"What?"

"Let's make this look as good as we can. Get some uniforms down here to walk around the scene and get a tow truck to pull my car. There's bound to be at least one set of eyes out there waiting this thing out."

"Good thinking buddy. Sure thing", Akers said. "Let me go make some calls and we'll get right on that. See ya' later" and he turned and left the room.

"Ok super sleuth, now what?" asked Sarah.

"What do you mean, 'now what'?"

"If you can't drive your car how are you going back to your apartment? Or your office? And they're probably watching those too."

"Oh yea. I guess you're right."

"You guess I'm right? Of course I'm right. So now what?"

"I haven't thought that far ahead yet."

"Well, I have. You're coming to my place."

"What?"

"You heard me. We'll wait until dark, get in my car which is parked in front, and go to my apartment."

"You can't-"

"I can do any damn thing I please Frank. Besides, it'll only be for a night or two and we should have this little issue bottled up."

"Well-"

"Well, I'm leaving now and I'll be back in about an hour or so. Be ready."

"Alright then. See ya' later", I said.

Nightfall came and from a side service entrance that is rarely used I could see a pair of headlights pull around. Sarah stopped within a few feet in the adjacent alleyway and turned the headlights off and on four times. Then the car went completely dark. I ran to the passenger side, quickly got in, and we were moving before I could close the door.

"In a hurry?" I asked.

"As a matter of fact, yes. I don't feel like drawing attention or getting shot. How about you?"

"Never mind."

As we sped along back toward mid-town the conversation abated for some time. I wasn't sure if things would mellow in a while or it was the calm before the storm. I couldn't quite pin down the personality. I'm sure that was her goal. And to give credit, she was moving through traffic at a pretty brisk pace and with considerable skill. If someone were trying to follow us they didn't stand a chance.

While enjoying the ride and being tossed about I struggled for a smoke. When I got the pack out and shook out a cigarette Sarah quickly glanced over.

"No", she said.

I looked over at her and replied, "No what?"

"No smoking. Not in my car."

I knew how to pick and choose my battles. I put it back in the pack. "So when do we get there? We've been driving around long enough to be in Jersey City."

"How did you know? That's where we're going. I have a friend who lives there and said we can use her house. She's in Europe now and no one is there so we'll have it to ourselves."

"How cozy."

"And I brought all the files so we can keep working. I also picked up some clothes and things for you."

"Oh, you did? How'd you get in my place?"

"Do you really want to know?"

"I guess I don't."

"A 'thank you' would be nice though", she said.

"I suppose it would be. And much deserved as well. Thank you", I answered. Just about that time the iron works of a skeletal bridge appeared and we were traversing the Hackensack River. "Wait... a... minute. Where are we? Isn't this the Pulaski Skyway? I thought we were going to Jersey City."

"We are. Did you think we were just going to hit the Holland Tunnel and pull up to the house? Come on. I'm making damn sure no one is following. Just relax. I'll hook back through Kearny, through Lincoln Park, and then back over to Little Italy. My friend's place is not far from St. Bridget's", she said.

"Alright. You're right. Thanks. I guess I am a little punchy. You think of everything. I should have known."

"Forget it. I'm nervous too. I'm sure it's even worse for you. These guys don't typically give up so we have to go on the offensive and fire back to stop it. Just running and hiding won't get it."

"I know."

It wasn't long before we were moving east along Montgomery Street. We passed an Esso station and I could see St. Bridget's church. It was late now and no other traffic could be seen. It had become a virtual ghost town. Knowing we were the only thing moving about made me even more nervous. Blending into a lot of traffic seemed much safer. "Are we there yet? There's the church", I said.

"As a matter of fact, we are. Just past the church up on the right. I think I'll turn right here on Brunswick and drop you in the back. There is a service entrance and it should be open. If we do still have a shadow they'll only see me park across from the building and walk in alone."

"Sounds like a plan", I said as Sarah put her shoulder into the steering wheel. No sooner had we made the turn onto Brunswick she started cranking hard back to the left and we arched into the alley. So far so good. About midway along the alley the car gradually slowed. We were both scanning the area intently but saw nothing. The car stopped. "There", she said, pointing to a doorway to the left with one beat up dim light fixture overhead. I bailed and she pulled away. Before leaving the shadows I stood quiet for some time taking in all the sights and sounds. You could hear Sarah's car off in the distance but otherwise you could have heard a pin drop. It was too quiet. I finally made my way into the building without incident.

After a little while I made it to the fourth floor. The building was very close in style to the brownstones over in Manhattan. Not a bad place considering where we were. I found the apartment and the door was slightly ajar. Sarah had gotten there ahead of me. As I slowly pushed the door further open I could hear a radio although the volume was very low. "Sarah!?"

Without saying anything she leaned over and I saw her at the other end of the short hallway leading from the door to the expanse of the living room. She had only just arrived ahead of me and was hanging up her coat. I closed the door behind me and started to take my coat off as well.

"Well, I see you made it in one piece", she said.

"I was starting to wonder", I said as I continued into the parlor. I stopped to hang my coat and hat next to the entrance. "Nice place", I said as I turned from the coat hooks and looked around. Sarah was at the nearby hide away kitchen making coffee.

"How do you want your coffee?"

"Just black, thanks."

"I'll be just a minute. Go ahead and have a seat. I'll bring it out", she said.

I made my way over to the sofa. Along the way I made sure the blinds and drapes were closed. I could hear the faint sounds of a radio broadcast, the clinking of coffee cups and saucers, and a drawer sliding open accompanied by the rattling of loose flatware banging together. Sarah apparently took her coffee with embellishments. In short order she walked into the room carrying a cup on a saucer in each hand. Bending over and placing one on the coffee table in front of me she said, "Here, let me know if you need anything else" as our gaze actually met for the first time. Looking up into her cobalt blue eyes seemed to last a little longer than the usual glance. Her stare did not avert either.

After a moment she stood back up and walked to the other end of the sofa, placed her coffee on the table, and sat down on the sofa as well. By now I had my cup in hand taking my first sips of the hot beverage. Strong, like I liked it. She knew how to make coffee too.

"We can stay here as long as we need to until things settle down a little", she said.

"Some friend you have there."

"Like I told you, she's in Europe now and the plans are for her to tour around over there for about two weeks. She has a new friend who likes her very much."

"Oh, I see. And has a little money too. Well, good for her."

"It would seem. I brought the files along like I said but tonight we're through with work. Now is the time to just unwind. We'll get all that out tomorrow. It's been quite a taxing day or two. For me too."

"Oh?'

"Yes."

"What else has been going on?" I asked.

"Frank-", she answered with a pause. Placing her cup back on the saucer she turned back and looked at me. Still not speaking she moved over closer to me.

18

"So this is the list of names of everyone connected to all the victims' court cases", said Sarah as she raised her coffee cup.

"I have to admit that is a job well done. It makes me wonder why no one else has caught that by now. So let's recap before going off in every direction on this", I said.

Sarah began to run down the list again she'd compiled of everyone with a specific connection in common with each of our murder victims' most recent court cases. The ones where they had been the defendant. And each had been exonerated or found not guilty. As she read off the Who's Who of this Hit Parade I walked back to the kitchen to refill my coffee. The sun shone brightly through the small kitchen window and I was about to get hungry too. As she called the final name and their involvement I turned to look back across the room. "Are you getting hungry yet?"

Slightly lowering the paper and looking back at me over her glasses she smiled and said, "I thought you'd never ask. I'm famished. What did you have in mind?"

"After last night... whatever you'd like."

She placed the paper on the coffee table and rose to her feet. "Let's see what's here", she said as she stepped around the table and walked my way.

oOo

It was early the following morning Sarah dropped me off back in mid-town about a block from my apartment. It was barely daylight and traffic was light. As soon as I stepped out of the car she sped away. I moved back away from the curb and stood momentarily with my back against the brick wall. I just stood, listened, and watched. Pedestrian traffic was virtually non-existent but the vehicle traffic was respectable. I finally felt it was safe to walk on.

When I got home I walked around to see if my car was there. It was. Calvin followed through again. I knew he would. After spending a while slowly checking it out, it too appeared clean. I guess the boys bought the ruse they got me. I headed upstairs to see if they left the apartment alone too.

When I was satisfied no one had been in my apartment I telephone Lieutenant Akers. I had been 'out of pocket' for a couple of days and I needed to catch up.

"Lieutenant Akers, what can I do you for?"

"Calvin? Frank."

"Frank!? Is that you?"

"I just said it was. Are you daft or something? I need to get up with you."

"Where are you?" Akers asked.

"I'm home. Just got here a little while ago but I'm about to pull out."

"Look, I'm about to leave. I'll drop by."

"Alright then. I guess I'll hang my hat back up and start some coffee."

"Good. See you in a few", he said and then came the loud click of him hanging up on me. When the line was clear I tried calling Sarah.

oOo

Walking back into the parlor from the kitchen I heard a short but loud knock at the door. I recognized it as being Akers. A short detour and I had the door open.

"Come in Cal", I said as I turned away from him and headed back to the kitchen. Akers entered my apartment and followed me after he pulled the door shut. "Coffee?" I asked.

"Sure thing Frank. Look, I really need to let you know I think we found the guy who shot at you the other day."

"Oh really?"

"Well, actually, he was ID'd and he's being held. What I really needed to let you know is who he is."

"Ok Calvin, who is he?"

"That's not what I mean Frank."

"Are you ok Calvin? You sound like a crazy person. What the hell are you trying to say?"

"Look Frank, I just spoke to Ellison yesterday. The Feds ID'd this cat for us. It's somebody associated with the German Embassy. The gun he used was a new German K98 Mauser carbine. The shooter was sloppy and left a spent 8mm cartridge in his sniper nest. It's a long story but Ellison's boys found that and the gun to match it still in possession of the shooter. So we have the gun, casing, and your friend all on ice."

"Well done Calvin. Ellison's crew are on the ball. So why shoot me?"

"They're still working that one out but the best we can figure is it has something to do with McAghon and the lady who keeps coming around the Pit fishing for info about him. It all ties in together with a group of Nazi Intelligence Operators that has yet to be completely identified. Look, I'm not supposed to know any of this and if it gets out I've been talking to you about it, it could be my job. Or even worse."

"Your secret is safe. Thanks for the heads up. So maybe some of these Nazi guys think I have something on them because of McAghon's lady friend so they'll just shut me up?"

"The good part is they think they did. At least for now until you re-surface."

"So what's up with the other Dead Club members? What's their connection?" I asked.

"I'm not sure. I haven't really been able to patch that one."

"Kinda' important isn't it? We have four other guys killed exactly the same way. What the hell Calvin?"

"I know, I know."

"Nazis didn't kill them all. Or if they did then, why? We have a plumber, a counter clerk, real estate salesman, and family doctor, none of whom knew the others and all killed the same as McAghon. If the Nazis didn't know and kill them all we're back to square one, now aren't we?"

"I see your point Frank."

"Look Calvin, we can keep chasing these leads on this end like you've been doing. Sarah is chasing down some other things I don't think are connected to the Nazis. In fact she told me she was heading out of town for a few days. There were a few things she needed to check out in Philly."

"Philadelphia?"

"Right. It's only a hundred miles away. I think she may really be on to something."

"Like what Frank?"

oOo

After a while Lieutenant Akers called into his office from my place before deciding to head out. Checking in, he was told about another murder. The body of a well-dressed man had been found washed up on Hart Island.

"Thanks. I'll head straight over from here. Bye", Akers said into the receiver before placing it back into its cradle.

"Sounds like job security for you Calvin."

"Yeah, and for you too buddy. Get your coat and hat. You're coming with me."

"Oh?"

"Yeah. This guy is too well-heeled to be part of Hart Island. He floated there from somewhere else and I have a feeling this may be connected to all this other stuff."

"I'm game. Let's go", I said picking up my hat on the way to the door. Akers had already opened it and was in the hall before I could grab my coat. Catching up to him I could hear him still mumbling. He was busy telling me something but he forgot I wasn't there.

"Calvin, hold on a minute. Settle down. If he's dead it's not an emergency. He'll still be there when we get there." I caught up to him at the elevator. "Now, start over. I didn't catch anything after you walked out in the hall."

The elevator arrived and I opened the door. As we stepped on Akers started again. I turned to close the door and pull the gate. "The guy still had his wallet and money", he said as I pushed the button.

"So it's not a robbery."

"No. Sounds like a hit. Has his watch and everything. They took nothing."

"Sounds like it."

"And, according to his ID his name is Jonathan Stephens."

"The attorney?"

"With Cromwell and Sterling. Yes. The same one", answered Akers.

"So what's got your tail feathers on fire? Somebody killed a lawyer. From a firm who basically handles top shelf clientele."

"He was stabbed with a large pair of scissors", Akers answered. I froze in place. After a moment I surmised, "How could it be connected? He's dressed and washed up on Hart Island. It doesn't mesh."

"You're right except for one thing."

"What?"

"According to Davis the scissors in Stephens are J. Wiss & Sons Model 'A' Pinking Shears. They're huge and heavy. Almost a foot long with black handles. Not to mention this is the exact make and model of sewing scissors found in each and every member of the Dead Club."

"Are you serious?"

"So you tell me Holmes, what are the odds?"

"I know. They are fairly common and popular in sewing circles but I get your point. Do you think the M.O. has changed? You know that doesn't happen."

"It doesn't usually happen. But it could", Akers countered.

"Rarely, but you're right again", I said.

Lieutenant Akers and I traveled up to the crime scene and actually met the transporting ambulance coming off of City Island. Davis and the other homicide dicks were right behind the wagon so we had a chance to talk to those guys at the same time.

"So lieutenant we found this dinner check from the Glen Island Casino in New Rochelle and a room key at the Glenwood Inn in his pockets. It looks like he had company up there if you know what I mean", said Davis.

While Davis talked we looked over the body. Calvin even confirmed the style of weapon to be a match with the others. Calvin looked so engrossed with examining the body it appeared he heard nothing. But he heard everything. When Davis finished Akers extended his left arm straight out toward Davis with his palm up and hand opened. "I'll take those", he said.

"Sir?"

"You heard me. I'll take those things from Glen Island. You guys go on down to the Pit and finish up your reports. We're heading on up there now to get a jump on this."

"Yes sir."

As the wagon and the boys pulled away and back onto the roadway Calvin held the room key tag with both hands and stared intently at it as if he were actually reading the print on it.

"So what are you thinking Calvin?"

"It's a straight shot from Glen Island to here along Long Island Sound. This key I'm holding could be the best break we've gotten so far. Let's go."

After some time we were motoring up Shore Road. Where it met Weyman Avenue we made the turn onto the Glen Island Approach. After crossing over onto Neptune Island we saw a sign directing us to turn left. Calvin eased off the accelerator and the sound of the engine's rpm's all but went silent.

"That sign said here, right?" he asked me.

"Yea Calvin. Left here."

Lieutenant Akers pushed in the clutch, shoved the gear shift straight up into second, and turned the wheel hard left barely slowing down. Almost through the turn onto Harbor Lane he eased down on the gas and up on the clutch pedal and the roar of the engine set us back in our seats again. He quickly put it back in third and we were back up to speed.

"I'm glad you know where we're going", I said.

"I don't. But it shouldn't be too hard to find. Not much out here."

With that we were coming up on a stop sign. The road did not continue but gave us the choice of a left or right turn. "Well?" asked Akers.

"Go right. There's not much left out that way. If it's wrong we'll find it soon enough without much more searching. Besides, the address is on Fort Slocum Road. Either way we'll be there in a few minutes."

Akers turned the wheel to the right and eased out on the clutch pedal again. We made the turn and no sooner did he make it back to third gear we saw the green lit 'Vacancy' sign ahead.

"There. Up on the right", I said while pointing.

"I see it", he replied.

We turned into the motor lodge with the engine nearly silent and not pulling. Akers coasted into a parking space right in front of the office. Pushing the shifter up into reverse he reached out and turned the key back. The engine went silent and he reached down with his left hand to pull the brake handle up. "Let's go see what's up", he said as he pulled the key out and opened the door.

"Right behind you Cal", I answered as I pushed open my door.

Lieutenant Akers seemed to be in a bit of a rush. He was already walking around the front end of the sedan when my door made the tell-tale solid thud sound of closing. Once past the front of the parked car he made a left onto the walkway leading to the office. I was following by almost ten feet. Approaching the office one could tell it was merely a converted cabin the same as all the rest on the property. The green neon 'Vacancy' light shone bright leaning against the inside of the front window. Its brightness was accentuated by the growing darkness provided by the sun sliding below the horizon. The door was still unlocked so we were able to walk in as a regular guest. A small brass bell attached to a piece of spring steel had been strategically placed above the door to alert anyone inside there was a visitor. A gentleman of about forty years was seated on a padded stool behind a counter next to the cash register. He was trained on the door before we even opened it completely and were walking in.

"May I help you gentlemen?" he asked as Akers turned to push the door shut. I had stepped in behind him and continued around to the counter as Cal pushed the door and the metallic clicking sound of the latch engaging could be heard. The little bell above the door, although silent now, still danced about as if it were trying. A radio could be heard but the volume was so low you couldn't make out the program or even where it was.

"Good evening. My name is DeGrae. Frank DeGrae. I'm a private detective and I'm working with the Police Department on a few things", I said as Akers walked up. "And this is Lieutenant Calvin Akers with the NYPD. We just needed a minute of your time if that's alright?"

Extending his hand toward the shop keeper Akers continued with, "That's right sir. Lieutenant Akers, glad to meet you." As the clerk reached to shake hands, Akers continued. "We just wanted to ask a few questions about one of your guests and then we'll be on our way."

"Sure thing lieutenant. Anything you guys need. I'll be glad to help."

Akers opened a file folder, holding only a few things as yet, and took out the driver license of our friend Jonathan Stephens. Holding the cabin key in his left hand he placed the ID on the counter and pushed it across with his free hand. "Do you remember this guy being here?"

"He looks familiar. Hold on", he said reaching for the guest register. "I think he was just here recently."

"He was. Last night", Akers said. The clerk looked up from his book with his eyes now wide.

"Yes! I remember. He looked very well dressed but came in alone. We didn't see anyone else in his car either. It seemed a little odd. Hold on", he finished and went back to thumbing through the register. "Here. Here he is. He signed in as 'John Smith' and took bungalow 4."

"Is anyone in there now?" I asked.

"I don't suppose. This shows he still has it. And the key hasn't been returned either."

Akers held the key up by its fob. As it dangled he said, "I have it. Bungalow 4 is now a crime scene. We're going to take a look and you tell everyone working here no one goes in there until we're finished."

"Oh, yes sir", he answered.

As we started for the door I stopped and turned back, "Oh yes, did you manage to see anything else going on with this fellow? I mean, you did think enough to have someone look in his car for other room guests. He didn't by chance have a visitor meet with him later, did he?"

"Oh yes!" he said with heightened excitement. "I almost forgot. Thanks for reminding me."

"Well?" I asked as Akers came back inside.

"Well you see, he came in kind of late. Oh, about 10:00 PM or so but about an hour later, after he was already over there and settled in, we did see a little white sports car pull in and go park next to his car." After a brief moment of reflection he continued, "Yes, that's right. A small car about an hour later. We didn't see who got out and went inside but early this morning we did see a rather fetching young lady drive out of here in it. She was alone. I guess it's the same person who snuck in here to meet him."

"Did you see what kind of car it was?"

"We don't like to pry on our guests and I feel whatever they do is their own private business."

"Did you see the car? What kind was it?"

"Well, it did seem a little exotic so I walked over... just to appreciate the vehicle mind you... and I think it was a BMW 328."

"A BMW 328? Are you sure?"

"That's what the badging said. I think. I've never seen one before. It's very small and only has two seats. A little sportster. Very nice."

"You, by chance, didn't notice the license plate did you?"

"Not really. Since she didn't stop in here I don't have it on the register. But I do seem to remember it looked a little different. It was a little dark but I think it may have even been foreign. European maybe. But that doesn't make sense", he said.

I said, "Yea, you're right. It doesn't. But thanks for all your help" as we stepped outside.

As Akers and I walked across the tightly packed pea-gravel parking lot I asked, "So any guesses as to who the German girl is who met him up here?"

"German?"

"Oh come on now. All this embassy and Nazi stuff and me being shot at with a Mauser and now this. A BMW with a European looking tag on it?"

"You're probably right but we can't jump to conclusions", Akers replied.

"Alright then. How's this for jumping to conclusions? A large pair of J. Wiss & Sons Model 'A' Pinking Shears added to the mix."

"You've made your point and those are the leads we're running down first. Damn I hate it when you're right."

"Yea you hate it. That's why I'm here with you now. Let's check out this cottage."

oOo

After Akers and I checked out Bungalow #4 only to find a bloody mess and rope it off for investigators I finally got back home near midnight. When I turned off the bedside lamp and my head finally sank in the pillow my phone rang. I reached over, grabbed the receiver from the hook, and yelled out, "What!?" Bringing the receiver to my ear I could make out Sarah's voice. I sat back up and turned the lamp back on. I picked up the rest of the phone and brought it closer to my face. "Now, what? I couldn't hear you very well."

"I said I was beginning to worry about you. I've been calling since this afternoon."

"Where are you?"

"I'm back in New York with a little news."

"Alright. Look, Akers and I just got back to Manhattan from New Rochelle this evening. I've got plenty to drop on you too. Be here... or rather... meet me at the office in the morning and we'll sort through all this new stuff. I'm going to bed now. Bye."

"Okay Frank. See you tomorrow."

19

Sitting at my desk I closed the folder, slid it to one side, and looked up to see Sarah sitting and staring back. "Well?" she said.

"This is some amazing stuff you dug up. I'm not entirely sure just yet but I think you might have it here."

"So what happened up in New Rochelle?"

Just as we were about to get into everything Akers and I did yesterday the phone rang. "DeGrae Detective Agency", I said into the phone after snapping it up.

"Frank?"

"Calvin? Is that you?"

"Frank. One of our patrol guys found that little BMW parked near the cruise liner piers this morning. You need to get down there and see what's up. I'm coming too but I know you can get there a lot faster than me."

"On it Cal."

"And here's a big surprise. It's parked across the street from where you and Sarah almost got in trouble. Do I need say more?"

"Thanks. We're heading that way now." I dropped the phone in its cradle and rose to get my coat and hat. Walking around from behind the desk I said, "Let's go. That was Akers. We're heading back to the piers."

"The cruise ship pier? The same pier as before?"

"That's the one. I'll fill you in on the way. Same stuff I was about to tell you before Akers just cut in."

"This just keeps getting better all the time", she said while grabbing her purse.

As we cruised along the mid-town streets discussing the previous day's events in New Rochelle I pointed out, "So I know there was a third party there. Probably a setup. A hit."

"So you think even with the physical evidence of the shears the Nazi government is involved at some level?"

"I'm not ready at this point to name names and positively connect the dots but I think we're very close. And when we get down here it may very well answer many more questions. Akers told me the New Rochelle mystery car is supposed by down here. In fact it should be in this area. Keep a sharp eye out for a small two-seater BMW roadster."

"Up there", Sarah said. I looked over to see her pointing straight ahead. "See the cop double parked up there? He's still with it."

"Oh yes. So there it is", I said in a satisfied sort of tone as I eased my Chevy coupe to a stop directly behind the patrol unit. The cop was standing on the sidewalk near the passenger side of the car in question.

As we walked up to him, he looked up from his notepad in our direction. His facial expression said it all. A master of non-verbal communication. "No officer, this is not our car. I'm DeGrae and I'm to meet Lieutenant Akers here. This is my associate Sarah Landers. I was out with Akers on the homicide case in New Rochelle last night."

His face instantly morphed into a much softer and pleasant countenance as he responded, "Oh yes Mr. DeGrae. How are you, sir?"

"Well, thank you. So, do we know anything more about this car? Has the registration told us anything?"

"Well, sir, not much. According to the registration it's a 1937 BMW 328 registered to a Jonathan Stephens with an address on Central Park West. Here, this was in the glove box", he answered as he held out a stack of folded papers.

"Did you say Jonathan Stephens?" I asked as I took the documents and started unfolding them. As I focused on the vehicle registration I saw the name in print as I heard, "Yes sir. Jonathan Stephens."

"I see. Thank you officer." I turned to Sarah and said a bit more quietly, "The suspect car comes back to the victim."

"I thought that's what I was understanding."

"What do you make of that?"

"A woman meeting a man away from town at a hotel driving a car owned by the man she's meeting. Duh. What do you think is going on?"

"A motor lodge."

"What?"

"It was a motor lodge with cabins. Not a hotel."

"Who gives a damn about that Frank? Are you losing it? A woman meets a man on the sly and she's driving his car. Don't you think they know each other? I mean know each other well?"

"Yes."

"Yes, what?"

"Oh please, Sarah. Enough already. Yes, they were a thing. This is personal. I'm beginning to think all these scissor murders have a personal element to them. I can't quite figure the connection to the Germans though. I'm going to park the car. You can come along or hang out here. I'm coming back. I need to see Akers before we take off."

"I'm coming."

Traffic was light down at the river. Even the liner piers were pretty sparse right now so it didn't take long to circle the block and find a space. When we turned the corner walking back I spotted a woman standing near the BMW talking with Officer Richards. "Look", I said to Sarah and stopped walking. I pushed Sarah away from the curb and against the corner shop wall. We both continued to spy the woman and cop standing next to the car.

"Is that her?" asked Sarah.

"Not only is that her, but that's one of the girls working for Marion McKinley."

"McKinley? The D.A.?"

"How do you know her?" I asked.

"I've met her but I also remember seeing her name all over these case files too. So who's this girl?"

"I don't know her name but I've seen her up in the D.A.s office every time I've gone up there. That's her. We've got to follow up on this one."

"Ok Frank. I'm going to cross the street-"

"No Sarah. She may recognize my face. Especially if I'm alone. If she catches a look at me and I'm walking alone it's a sure bet she'll look at my face but if we're walking as a couple... not so likely."

Sarah turned and took my arm in hers. "I'll play along." We stood turned toward the store front window as they continued talking at the car. As the two continued their conversation Akers and Jimmy Little pulled up and parked just as I had earlier and got out. The young lady kept her composure as Akers and Little walked up into their conversation. With the four of them in conference it was going to be interesting to see what comes next.

Sarah glanced over her shoulder taking in the scene. Looking back into the reflection of the window she said, "This should be entertaining."

"My thoughts exactly."

Almost as soon as I answered Sarah our girl started walking on down the sidewalk. When she moved further away Sarah and I started for the parked BMW. Still several feet away I called out, "Calvin."

Akers turned his attention to my direction and when he saw us, "Frank. And Miss Landers. What a nice surprise."

"Calvin, did you guys get her name?"

"Her?" he said pointing back along the sidewalk toward our girl with his thumb.

"Yea. Her. The girl that just stepped away." I pointed straight through Akers and added, "That girl right there crossing the street in the crosswalk." There was no danger of getting burned now. She was about forty yards away and had her back to us.

"She's nobody really. She works up in the D.A.s office as a secretary or clerk or something. She stopped to ask about the car because she used to work for Spencer. She said she thought it may be his. Recognized it from some time back when he was driving it. Or one like it. They're not very common."

"Fine Calvin. What is her name?'

"Uh, Waters I think. Yea, something Waters. I can't remember her first name."

The beat cop looking at his notepad and Sarah fanning through papers in her folder answered simultaneously, "Bonnie." Akers looked at the cop and I turned to Sarah.

"Bonnie?" I asked Sarah.

"She's on my list of court case participants. Bonnie Waters. Not a major player but has been connected. Just in an administrative way from the prosecutor's office but she has had her fingerprint on all the court files. She does case prep, filing, and etcetera."

Akers looking back at us asked, "What are you talking about?"

"Probably nothing but one of our small loose strings", I said.

"Sounds like it could be more than a loose string."

"Well Calvin, you're stuck with this car doing cop stuff. Me and Sarah are heading across the street to see where Miss Bonnie Waters is going. I'll call you later." Sarah and I high stepped it across the street right there in the middle of the block.

Still trotting across the street I asked Sarah, "So where did she go? I know you were watching her while I chatted up the guys."

"I did. She turned into that liner terminal just the other side of the crosswalk."

When we got to the sidewalk I pointed ahead saying, "That one? You do remember this place?"

"I do."

"Alright then. Let's check it out", I said as we approached an opening between terminals. "Look. The Bremen is docked. Looks like people going up and down the gangways too."

"That's probably where she's headed", Sarah replied.

We stepped up the pace and filed into the terminal with what seemed like half the city's population. I had never seen a passenger terminal so congested. "Is there something going on I don't know about?"

"I have no idea. But the good news is with this many people packed in here we'll never be noticed."

Once inside the massive structure we kept to the right side since this was the side the Bremen was docked. The length was such you couldn't see the end. It was as if the building continued into infinity and the open atrium style to the roof shown all levels of entry to the docked ship just on the other side of the wall. The entire thing was so immense but seemed to consist of nothing more than ornate iron works and glass. Lots of glass to let the natural light come in to illuminate an otherwise huge and dark place. With the activity of this scale it reminded one of a kicked over ant hill.

"We need a plan to help figure out where she went. Guessing is not going to get it", I said over the steady hum of the moving crowd.

"Alright. Look. See that ticket station over there?"

"Yes", I answered.

"There should be a passenger manifest at each of these posts along here. That one only has one ticket agent."

"Check."

"Well then... I'll go up and, well, you know... get his attention. When I do you check that list."

"Let's go."

As we walked over I moved off to the right and Sarah continued straight ahead to the ticket counter. She also un-did a couple of buttons at the top of her blouse and tucked the corners in. If she was blending into the crowd going unnoticed before, that just went out the window. I was far enough away and the din of the crowd was such that I couldn't make out a word of their conversation. But, it was obvious her plan was working. The poor guy was fixated on Sarah's, um, shirt collar. In short order she managed to lure him from behind the counter and they disappeared off into the crowd. This was my cue.

oOo

Walking through the crowded terminal I said, "Great job, Sarah. I don't know what you said to that guy but it sure worked. And I did see her name. She's using her real name. Sure makes things easy for us except for one thing."

"What's that?"

"She's actually on the passenger list. She's a passenger. We really need to play this out. We've got to know where she's going and why."

"You mean-"

"We've got to take a cruise Sarah."

"I can't just hop on a boat like that. I've got to-"

"We've got to go. And we've got to go now."

"You go. It doesn't take both of us to watch her. Where can she go on a boat anyway?" she said.

"I need you to go with me. It'll take us both. We need to watch her all the time. Who is she going to meet? Who will she be seen with? Where will she get off? It goes on and on. And we can run smoke and mirrors for each other posing as a married couple interested in nothing but each other."

"What about clothes and things? We have nothing but the clothes we're wearing."

"We'll manage. It's part of the game to move on the fly. You know that", I said to her. "Here, take the keys and run back to the car. Get your purse-. You do have a passport don't you?"

"Yes."

"With you? In your purse?"

"Well, yes, I do carry it in my purse."

"Good. Grab it and a small black duffle in the trunk. It's my emergency go bag. While you're doing that I'll buy tickets. I'll meet you at the first ticket counter and we'll board together. Run." She took off for the door to the street without another word.

oOo

Having cleared the slip and starting down the Hudson, Sarah and I stood quietly at the railing taking in the sights and sounds of departing New York as passengers on an ocean liner bound for new adventures. It was exciting at that. The tugs had managed to get us in the channel and moving along quite well. People were cheering and waving and the ship's horn sounded periodically. I could see the Statue of Liberty in the distance and then was reminded we were on a German KdF ship flying the Nazi swastika flag. The whole affair seemed surreal.

"So Frank, what are we going to do about sleeping arrangements?"

"What do you mean?"

"Our stateroom is small. Very small with one bed in it."

"What do expect me to do about it? We'll just have to deal with it. You're a big girl. It's all part of the persona that we're a married couple. Play the role."

"Play the role?"

"Play the role."

"Alright. You asked for it. I'll play the role", she said as she grabbed me by the lapels and pulled me in for a rather long kiss. Finishing and pushing me back she asked, "Do you think that was convincing?"

"I'll let you know. We may have to work on it", I answered as I straightened my jacket.

"So, what about sleeping? Do we sleep in shifts or actually share the bed?"

"I don't know about you but I'm going to bed when I get tired. You can do whatever you please. Sleep with me or sleep alone. I don't care. Right now I'm going to find something to eat. Hungry?"

"Well, now that you mention it, I guess I could eat something."

"Well let's go find where the food is", I said.

We found Miss Bonnie Waters in short order and for almost two days she was monitored without incident. She didn't do anything nor was she seen speaking with anyone longer than it took to ask for the time. Time would tell if this snap decision to sail was a good idea or not. As far as an impromptu vacation and chance to get Sarah alone was an entirely different matter.

With only two days into a ten-day voyage we began to shadow Miss Waters in varying modes of disguise. Some of the time we split the day with solo runs and others we accompanied one another in our guise as a married couple. And being on a ship made surveillance very easy as we never had to get close. There was nowhere to go. We couldn't lose her. And we knew where her stateroom was so this surveillance job was like shooting fish in a barrel. More time passed and still we never saw her even speak to anyone.

Walking the deck at midday the sun gave the appearance of becoming a little larger and a little warmer although the temperature did remain comfortable due to the steady brisk breeze that never subsided. Looking out in every direction one was reminded of the old belief the Earth was flat and you could sail off the edge if not careful. Only now it looked the same in every direction. You also lacked a sensation of movement until looking over the railing at the ship's hull. Looking over the side you suddenly felt as if you were riding on a huge speedboat. The bow seemed to slice effortlessly through the water and at great speed. The water pushed away from the steel with such force it churned to white caps to start creating a quite impressive wake that could be seen trailing for infinity.

"So, any ideas?"

"I don't know. I guess this wasn't such a good idea after all", I said.

Sarah just stopped and turned to stare at me. No particular expression could be read although many unpleasant versions ran through my head. I continued, "Sorry. I don't know what she's doing but I guarantee it's something. She didn't get on this boat simply for a pleasure cruise and she certainly isn't going on vacation alone."

Sarah looked back ahead and started to move again. "I suppose you're right."

"I have noticed something else too. Or at least I think I have."

"Alright. What?" she said.

"We're not moving east. We're going south", I answered.

"What?"

"Right. I've been paying attention to how the sun has been traveling across the sky in relation to the position of the boat. It's been crossing our axis from left to right. We're moving south."

"Where are we going then?"

"Not a clue. We'll know when we get there. I've also noticed at night in the extreme distance what appears to be lights on the starboard horizon."

"Every night?" she asked.

"Every night. Or early in the morning before sunrise."

"So, what is that supposed to be?"

"Our eastern coastline. This ship has been moving south and staying just in view of the U.S. eastern seaboard. It's almost like they're mapping us."

"You've got to be kidding", she said.

"I don't think so. I'm thinking she's part of a much bigger picture here too. I'm not sure what it is yet. But something we need to get the FBI tuned into", I answered.

"Alright. Say this thing is spying on us. How do we let the Feds know what's going on?"

"I have no idea right now. But we have to figure something out pretty quick before we turn out into International Waters. For all we know they may have already passed some information off to a U-Boat and it's too late."

"Hey! I just remembered hearing about some new military goings-on around Virginia and the Carolinas. Do you think that's what they wanted to see?"

I replied, "Sure, they would love to see that stuff. And any other thing they may deem important. That's exactly the thing I was thinking about."

Sarah and I continued our stroll along the teakwood deck working our way forward on the starboard side. Although it was daylight out now and I couldn't really see anything but water looking to the western horizon I was always hopeful of seeing something. But nightfall would bring into view a whole new world again.

oOo

After a few days at sea I left the stateroom early in the morning in search for coffee. This whole cruise thing started to seem like a bad idea with nothing to show for it until today.

I made my way to the Lido Deck café and grabbed two cups of coffee to take back to the room when I noticed what looked to be the St. John's River Bridge in the distance accompanied by a much closer view of a shoreline. Of course! Jacksonville, Florida. We've been following the eastern U.S. Coastline and now stopping off in Florida. Still some time from going up river and reaching port I hurried back to the room as quickly as I could.

"Sarah!" I said as I entered the stateroom letting the door bounce off the bulkhead with a teeth jarring thud.

"What the...!" she cried out bolting upright from her slumber.

"Here's your coffee. Get up."

"Are you mad? Get out."

"Get up Sarah. We're approaching port."

"What port? Where are we?"

"Get up. Here's your coffee. I'll fill you in when you're awake and will remember what I tell you. We've got to find Miss Bonnie Waters too. And quick."

"What's the rush Frank?"

"I'm betting whatever she came onboard for has been done and she's getting off here to go back to New York. Just get up and get dressed and we'll cover all this then. I'll see you back up in the café", I said as I was stepping back out onto the deck.

Pulling the cabin door shut I heard the distinctive click of the latch catching and started my return trip back to the dining room. The foot traffic along the deck was noticeably picking up as well. It was, after all, time for the early risers to search out breakfast. Reaching the aft part of the main deck I found the port side interior stairs back to the Lido café and the buffet table set with all the Continental offerings. I kept it simple with a refill and onion bagel. Dipping a bit of cream cheese onto the saucer alongside the bagel I was set to find us a table. In surprising short order I spied Sarah entering the dining room as I was about to sit down. Rather than have her hunt for me I skipped the table and went to her.

As Sarah stood before the coffee urn drawing her refill I eased up directly behind her until close enough to whisper into her ear. "Hello there. Would you care to share a table?"

Without the slightest movement she continued filling the cup and answered, "You're a funny guy. I suppose I will at that." She finished with the urn and turned around. "Oh Frank, how nice of you to bring me a bagel. You should get something to eat too", she said as she reached out and took my plate.

"You're welcome", I replied as I released my grip. "I guess I will."

"Look."

"What?"

"There", Sarah said as she nodded toward the door I entered earlier. "Bonnie Waters."

"Well, well. This may be our lucky day after all. Now we don't have to hunt her down." Just as I and a hundred other passengers had done she approached the Continental buffet table and started filling a coffee cup. The surveillance game had begun.

By now almost everyone had settled down to chairs and tables enjoying their breakfasts as the ship drew closer the opening of the bay. There was no doubt we were heading for port in Jacksonville. Much to our surprise a gentleman made his way through the crowd and sat at Miss Waters' table with no conversation or hesitation. Once seated they immediately engaged in conversation. About six feet tall with a thin frame he appeared to be about thirty years old with sandy hair and a thin mustache. He wore wire framed glasses with his dark pinstriped suit and carried in luggage appearing to belong to both of them. His most distinctive feature was how familiar he seemed to her and we had not seen him until now.

"Alright, who goes for their belongings first? You or me?" I asked.

"I guess I will", Sarah answered.

"I'll be right here unless they move. Hurry back."

It turned out to be advantageous we were traveling light. The passengers took full advantage of the time docked and were going everywhere in a swirl of activity. We, of course, had to match our movements with Miss Waters and do it at a distance. We finally saw her actually disembark and she did so in the company of a young man. Since we had not actually watched her board the ship back in New York we did not know who he was. She was never seen with anyone during our days at sea. She curiously had no luggage either. Not even a carry-on bag. Only her purse. It seemed quite obvious her voyage was intended to be a short jaunt at that. Sarah and I departed the ship at an interval apart with Sarah going first and keeping Miss Waters in view. I followed Sarah at a distance I could see only her. It was as if we were running a relay. We thought it may be best not to be seen leaving together. If nothing else just to keep things mixed up a bit.

20

"So you see Calvin, this thing looks to be a little bigger than we thought. I wanted to run all this by you before we called Ellison", I said.

"So where is Waters now?" Lieutenant Akers asked.

"As far as we can tell she's back home at her apartment and resuming her normal routine as a clerk in the DA's office. It's as if nothing ever happened. You tell me. Who takes a quick cruise along the seaboard and grabs a train back to New York from Florida? Straight down and back up. No stopping. No sightseeing. Nothing."

"Okay Frank. I'll get with Ellison on this and you two stay on it. I'll let you know what's going on as soon as I do."

I left Calvin's office and headed for the lobby. Just as I got to the stairs an elevator stopped and opened. Hearing the ding of the bell and rumble of the opening door I unconsciously turned to look and who should step out but Marion McKinley and Sarah. As I approached the top step I did a double take in their direction and hesitated. The two of them seemed rather immersed in conversation and had not noticed me. I decided I wouldn't get between them and loitered around a bit in the hall. If Sarah was getting some good insight I certainly didn't want to interrupt that. I stepped over to the phone booth and pulled the door closed as I retrieved a nickel from my pocket.

oOo

It was late in the afternoon when I saw Sarah exit the building and start down the steps. I pulled the handle and pushed the door open as I stepped out. Sarah was reaching the bottom step when I walked to the front of my car and met her on the sidewalk. Looking up she came to a most abrupt stop with a rather surprised look on her face. "Frank!"

"Hi. So what's cooking?"

"What are you doing here?"

"I was working. Who did you come down here to see?"

"I saw a lot of people. What are you doing here? Waiting for me?"

"No. I just left meeting with Akers. He's going to brief the FBI on our little excursion. He told me he would update us on that situation and asked us to keep doing what we're doing. Seeing you here kept me from having to hunt you down."

"Well Frank, I just left the DA's office speaking with Miss McKinley. She told me she hasn't seen Bonnie Waters in almost a week."

"Oh, really?"

"But I did chat with a few other ladies in the office who told me she has been around this week. I guess McKinley just hasn't crossed paths with her."

"Don't you find that a little odd? I know Marion, I mean Miss McKinley, is fairly busy in and out of the office as an Assistant Prosecutor but doesn't Waters handle most of the case files there? Her name seems to appear on almost all of the briefs somewhere", I replied.

"To be honest, I don't know. I don't know their routine in there and for all I know Miss Waters could simply be a file clerk."

"Good point Sarah. Then I guess we need to look a little closer at Waters' routine. I'm going back in to see Akers for a minute and I'll see you tomorrow", I said as I turned back toward the steps.

"Alright Frank. See ya' in the morning", I heard from behind as I quickly ascended the stairs skipping every other step. Reaching the top tier and the massive doors I grabbed the large brass handle. Once again I was crossing the expanse of the marble tiled lobby but this time I stopped at the bank of elevators rather than going for the spiral staircase in the center of the atrium. The center door opened and I stepped aboard. The building being only four flights up and fairly heavy with foot traffic; the city installed automatic elevators just the year before. I turned toward the door and reached over to the panel and pressed '3'.

Just as I stepped off the elevator I suddenly had a thought. I quickly made my way over to the stairs and hurried back to Lieutenant Akers' office one floor down. Reaching the second floor landing I saw Akers standing in front of the elevators. I managed to find him just as he was leaving for the day.

"Calvin!"

Turning quickly toward me he answered, "Frank? What the-"

"What the hell is with taking the elevator down one floor?"

"Is that why you're here? Checking on my walking habits?"

"No, but maybe I need to. Let's go back to your office", I said and turned to go down the hall.

Trying to catch up Akers said, "Well, I guess we will."

I stopped and turned around. Akers looked up from the floor and quickly stopped facing me. "Calvin. I think I've just had an epiphany about this series of murders and a thought struck me as I was about to get in my car out back. We need to find a very safe place to go over this."

"My office should be alright. Wait a minute."

"Wait?"

"Never mind the office. Follow me."

"Right behind you."

We started back toward the atrium and I followed Calvin straight down the stairs. As we reached the bottom of the steps back to the parked cars he said, "Get in. We're going back to the diner. I've got a little something for you too so we'll make this an outing."

"Right", I answered already moving to the passenger side of his unmarked sedan. With the solid thud of both doors closing simultaneously Akers started the engine and looked over at me. "Ellison called back just a few minutes ago", he said.

"Oh? And?"

Akers shifted into Reverse and eased off the clutch. "You apparently just confirmed what they had been suspecting. It seems these so-called German civilian cruise liners are being used to map out our eastern coastline. It looks like our very own Miss Bonnie Waters may be involved to some degree but to what extent isn't quite known just yet."

"So where does that leave us?"

"I think the DA's office should know about her but Ellison told me to keep quiet. Any tip of the hand could disrupt what the Feds are doing. This also means if she winds up being any more involved in your investigation you'll need to back off. National Security trumps murder cases."

"I was afraid of something like this. Is there anyone in the DA's office we can trust to keep this close to the vest?" I asked.

"I'll have to sleep on that one. So, what did you have?"

Akers pulled to the curb just down from the automat and shifted back into Reverse as he shut the car off. As he eased up off the clutch pedal I opened my door and stepped out onto the sidewalk. I shut the door and walked to the front of the car as Lieutenant Akers' door closed. As he approached I answered, "I almost went to the DA's office when I made the last second decision to head down to see you. It would seem the best thing we've put together so far concerning the Dead Club is the victims are all connected through the DA's office because of being defendants in homicide cases themselves."

"What?"

"That's right. These guys have nothing else in common. Nothing. Where they live, where they work, how they spend their off-time, people they know, school history, nothing. Then Sarah started looking at their files as defendants in the DA's office. They have all been charged and tried for assaulting a wife or girlfriend who, in every case, died of their injuries at a later time. And in each case they were given probation or flat out found Not Guilty."

Akers pulled the bar on the shiny chrome and glass door and I passed him stepping inside. We went our separate ways once inside grabbing trays and checking out the offerings in their individual tiny windows. I thought the chicken salad sandwich looked especially good today.

I found Lieutenant Akers already at a table when I started moving about searching for a place to sit. Setting my tray on the table's edge and pulling back the chair he started in with, "So let me get this straight. The two of you have come to the conclusion the thread that ties these guys together is they have killed a significant other?"

"And been processed through the New York City's District Attorney's Office for prosecution."

"And they have been adjudicated and back out on the street", Akers finished.

"Correct."

"So what does all this have to do with Bonnie Waters and her trip to Florida?"

"Absolutely nothing."

"What?"

"That's right Calvin. Nothing. I do think there's a possibility she may be connected to the murders but I also think she may also be working with the German government somehow. And most probably, one has nothing to do with the other."

"So what's the plan?"

"Have you heard from Ellison yet?"

"No. Not yet. I guess we should get a feel from him what the Feds are up too. I sure don't want to jump the gun on anything and cause them problems. Get with Sarah and work out a plan to keep putting things together but stay out of sight. Really out of sight. We want everyone to relax a little whether it's a murder suspect or spies."

"I got it Cal. There's still plenty for us to do so I'll run her down when we leave here. I've got an idea about how to draw our killer out but I need to find out what Sarah's been up to first."

"Oh, you do? What are ya' thinking about Frank?"

"It's too early just yet but I'll get with you in a day or two with a plan", I replied as I pushed my chair back from the table. Pushing my chair back under the table I picked up my coffee cup. Akers pushed back from the table as I finished off my coffee.

"Frank, you've got to give me something. What if something happens?" Akers continued while stepping around the small table. I turned toward the door and we started back to the car.

Akers and I chatted on about the case and other things all the way back to his office. I finally decided it was time to go be productive again and was making my way out of the building when who should I meet near the second floor elevators but 'Officer' Cynthia Brant. I pondered over whether or not I should strike up a conversation since our last, and only, meeting had been so brief and very formal. So naturally I decided to press the issue with, "Well hello Officer Brant. How have you been?"

She stopped and replied, "Oh. Hello Mr. DeGrae. I've been well thank you. What brings you down here?"

"Oh, you remember me?"

"It's not hard. Everyone knows who you are. And that you used to work here with Lieutenant Akers. In fact, you're a bit of a celebrity around here."

"I see."

"Mr. DeGrae."

"Yes?"

"May I say something?"

"Please."

"I know I may have been a little abrupt-"

"Please. It's alright. I know how most men can be, especially to a woman in an unconventional occupation. I think I understand and no excuses or apologies are necessary."

There was a pause. A slightly awkward, albeit brief, silence. "Thank you Mr. DeGrae but that wasn't exactly what I was going to focus on."

"I apologize once again. So, what were you going to say?"

"Well sir, I was going to say although you may have thought I may be a little abrupt, or even abrasive, since I don't take much crap from too many people; I would like to let you know I would like to offer any help I may be able to give in your investigation."

"My investigation?"

"You are working on the murders with Lieutenant Akers, aren't you? At least the one where you and I met?"

"Well, yes. I am at that. Of course. And thanks for the offer. I may call you up for some help on this after all since you offered. Thanks."

"Well I'm heading up to the DA's office for a pre-trial meeting with an ADA. It was nice talking with you", she said as she turned and continued on her way.

I loitered enough until Brant was out of sight and walked over to the oak phone booth. I dialed up Sarah's apartment. Since it was so late in the day I was hoping she had made it home by now.

21

"Good morning Frank", Sarah blurted out as she entered the room. Catching me off guard, like she so often does, my head sprang up from reading a file.

"Oh. Hi. Bring coffee?"

"Good to see you too. As a matter of fact I did. That stuff you have around here tastes like stump water. When are you going to buy some real coffee Frank?"

"Why should I do that when I know you'll just bring some?"

"We have to talk more about this later. So what's on your mind?"

"I'm stuck on this 'DA's Office' thing. That seems to be the one thing that connects our victims and I'm starting to see the list of suspect names falling into place now."

"Waters?" Sarah asked.

"She's one, yes. But my imagination has added a couple of more possibilities. Have you met Cynthia Brant yet?"

"No. Should I have?"

"She's a rookie cop I met on the McAghon murder scene in mid-March. I bumped into her yesterday at the Police Building on her way to see an ADA for a pre-trial conference. What I don't know yet is if she was involved in the other cases and to what extent. I think we have some more foot work to do on that."

"We still have the criminal case files here in the office. I just kept them together in the bottom drawer of the barrister case."

"Give me Brody and Coley and you take Quarles and Duncan. I'll refill the coffee and donuts and then we can spend the morning combing through looking for any mention of Officer Brant."

"Frank, I just had an idea that might save us a little time", Sarah said while thumbing through the other four folders.

"Alright…"

"I just remembered these guys lived all over the map, right? I'm checking the addresses again now."

"Right."

"Brody lived on 5th Avenue. Coley, South Street. Quarles on East 54th Street, and Duncan, East 86th Street. Not to mention our last guy was staying at Central Park West."

"So where are you going with this?"

"Come on Frank. You were a cop. Are all these places on a single beat where the same uniformed cops would show up time after time?"

"Oh, I see it now. You're right."

"You need to check with your buddy Akers and find out if this Brant is on some special detail or squad and was called out on these crime scenes. And you did say she was on her way to the DA's satellite office in the Police Building, right?"

"Yes."

"Why?"

"For a pre-trial conference with an ADA", DeGrae and Landers said in unison while looking at one another.

"I get that Frank. For what, specifically? And wouldn't it be interesting to know which ADA. And we need to check who the prosecuting attorney was on all of them."

"You're right. We've been so focused on Bonnie Waters with all her strange and shady activity we may be overlooking something else. Ellison and the Feds are on her now anyway. Akers also told me he would keep us updated on what Ellison and his boys turn up on her. Let's slow it down a little and check all this other stuff."

Sarah and I divided the remaining four case file folders and settled in reading through them. We spent the better part of the day picking through each line until we were able to build outlines of who all the players were. Not long after lunch I made a call to Akers.

"Lieutenant Akers", he answered.

"Calvin. Frank."

"What's up Frank?"

"Can you tell me anything about a young rookie female officer by the name of Cynthia Brant?"

"An officer?"

"Right. She's a police officer."

"NYPD?"

"Yes Calvin. A New York City police officer. I met her in the lobby at the McAghon murder on Central Park West in mid-March. She brought me up from the lobby to the apartment."

"I don't know her. I can try to find out something though."

"She's a rookie. Been on just a couple of years. I remember her telling me she had been in the first group to take the new Policewoman test in '38. That should help a little."

"I'm sure it will", Akers replied and continued on with, "So when are you coming back down here? I'd rather discuss officers in person rather than on the phone."

"I understand. Not a problem. I'm thinking of paying Marion a visit so I can drop by then. I'll probably be by in the morning so I can catch her before she takes off for court the rest of the day."

"Marion? Marion McKinley?"

"Yes Calvin. Marion McKinley."

"After what I saw on the McAghon scene you want to see her?"

"No, I don't want to see her but she was the ADA on McAghon's homicide trial and the other Dead Club members' proceedings. I need to get her insight on this

Brant as well as Waters. And anything else she can give us."

First thing the next morning I made sure I was down at the DA's office in time to watch everyone show up for work. Including Marion and our Miss Bonnie Waters among the ranks. Calvin and I both suspected Waters of being a prime suspect and basically thought of her as a Nazi spy. That boat trip to Florida still bothered me. Sarah had traveled out to Philadelphia to check on a few things while I spent the day here.

When my Bulova Sky King showed 8:30 A.M. I pulled the keys from the ignition and pulled the door handle. Ascending the rear steps I paused for a moment and thought how nice it must be for Sarah to be heading out of the city to the simpler surroundings of the Philadelphia outskirts. The weather was perfect for anything outdoors. Looking up into the morning sky there was no hint of a cloud. A lone aircraft could be detected at a great distance off toward the Atlantic. It wasn't long before my feet set back onto the ground and I continued up to the entrance.

At the end of the hall on the third floor was a single large oak door with an opaque window in the upper half. A milky white wavy glass one could not see through with stenciling indicating this was the way into the District Attorney's office. I gripped the round brass door knob, turned it slightly, and pushed the incredibly heavy, yet balanced, door ever so slightly. It was as if I could quietly come in and not be noticed.

I turned to close the door behind me and could hear the steady hum of a large office in full swing. Filing cabinet drawers moving on their rollers and the clickety-clack of typewriters reverberated with a measure of power magnified by the number of machines operating. Mixed in was the occasional phone ringing and someone walking through appearing to be doing nothing in particular. I walked to the counter and simply stood watching the various activity play out in the large open gallery.

"May we help you?" was heard well before I could see where it came from. Then a young lady of about college age appeared. At first she gave the appearance of being a bit older dressed in business attire. Her dark hair was worn up and she had on cheaters. She almost looked a bit dowdy.

"Good morning miss. My name is Frank DeGrae and I was wondering if Miss McKinley could spare just a minute before she heads out to court?"

"May I ask what this is in reference to?"

"If you just give her my name she'll know."

"Alright. Mr. Frank…?"

"DeGrae. Frank DeGrae. Spelled 'D', small 'E', capital 'G', 'R', 'A', 'E'. DeGrae."

"Thank you Mr. DeGrae. If you'll have a seat over there I'll pass this on to her."

"Thank you", I replied as I stepped back to a small wooden bench against the wall near the door. I chose to continue standing and watched the clerk make her way through the serpentine course created by all the desks and work stations until she was no longer in view.

After quite a wait I was beginning to wonder if she was in the building when I saw her come into view. Emerging from where I last saw the young lady vanish on her way back I noticed Marion was wearing her jacket and carrying her purse and briefcase. She was even wearing a hat today. There was little doubt she intended to leave the building.

"Not today Frank. I'm really busy right now", she said without missing a beat. She pushed through the counter swinging door and continued toward the hall.

"Do I need to go see O'Dwyer then?" Marion stopped dead in her tracks and turned to face me. I stepped toward the door and around her emerging into the hallway ahead of her. I turned around to face her still framed in the doorway. "It's okay Marion. I'll go see your boss and I need to speak with Geoghan too since he was the boss last year when this crap started."

"Hold on Frank. I can spare five minutes. Let's go back to my office. I don't want to have this conversation out here."

"I didn't think you did. Lead the way."

Stepping into the inner sanctum of the McKinley lair she turned to me as I pulled the door closed starting in with, "Just who do you think you are marching in here-"

"For the record Marion I'm working directly for the Mayor and in concert with the NYPD and the Feds on this case. Do you really want me to play my hold cards?"

"What do you want Frank?"

oOo

"So we need to meet again when you get a little free time", I said.

"I can clear my calendar for anytime, Frank. Just let me know", replied Lieutenant Akers.

"Then we're more or less ready to roll this out? It's getting close to the time to add another name to the list. Make it look good Calvin. Say, oh about 2:00 A.M. or so?"

"You got it buddy."

"I guess we'll be on our way then. It'll be here before you know it", I said as Sarah and I rose from Calvin's office chairs. Calvin also stood from his seat behind the desk since there was a lady in the room too.

"It was nice to see you again too, Miss Landers."

"Thank you Lieutenant. You as well", answered Sarah as we moved toward the door.

With our golfing plans made, as well as our little outing for later tonight, I decided to head back to the office and call it a day. Tomorrow would start very early and it promised to be a very long but productive day. Before we made it to the car Sarah asked me again, "So who is it, Frank?"

Walking down the back steps with the parked cars in sight I asked, "You're asking me?"

"I know you've got some idea or this plan you two cooked up wouldn't be a scheduled operation yet."

I stopped on the sidewalk standing at the front of my car. We faced one another and I continued with, "Honestly, I don't really know yet. But I am sure that whoever it is will be there and we'll weed them out as it unfolds."

"Who do you think it is?"

"I can think of at least three solid suspects. Maybe even a fourth or fifth. I'm a little reluctant to name a single person right now so we don't develop tunnel vision and miss something. That's why I'm not giving you any specific name right now. I need you clear headed to keep me on track."

"I don't know if I should feel slighted or flattered. You're a funny guy, Frank."

"Thanks, Sarah. I think." After a slight pause I threw the ball back into her court. "You've worked on this thing as much as me. You must have some ideas."

"Well, I do as a matter of fact."

"Do you want to kick it around? Let's just make sure we don't color our opinion when we get this thing going."

"Where did I just come from and what did I find? That should answer that question."

"I must admit, that was some pretty convincing stuff."

22

It was 2:05 o'clock, ante meridiem, when the phone rang. Gradually the ringing grew louder until the bell sounded like a fire alarm. I stirred from the best sleep I'd had in ages and was a bit disoriented at first. Still discombobulated and quite irritated I managed to grab the receiver even in the dark.

"What!?" I shouted as I was still trying to wake up.

"Frank?" crackled a voice from across the wire.

"Who is it, Frank?" Sarah asked as she began stirring awake.

Holding my hand over the phone I answered, "It's Calvin. Hang on." I put the phone back to my ear. "Go ahead Calvin. You guys ready?"

"We are. And all the notifications have been made and most everyone is here. Nothing looks out of place or out of the ordinary so you rolling in after the fact shouldn't tip your hand."

"Alright. Sarah and I should be there in about an hour. Same place we discussed, right?"

"We're here. See you then."

I hung up the phone and reached for a smoke. Sarah was already walking around the foot of the bed and heading for the bathroom. I just sat on the edge of the bed and shook the last Camel from its crumpled pack as I watched the bathroom door close. Looking down at the smoke in one hand and the empty pack in the other I just tossed the empty back onto the night table and picked up the Zippo. Still holding an unlit cigarette I rose to go start a pot of coffee.

Walking into the kitchen Sarah asked, "So we have another murder victim, do we?"

"We do indeed. Mr. Andrew Holland is lying face down in the middle of the bed with a huge pair of sewing shears sunk between the shoulder blades. It's show time." Sarah smiled as she poured her coffee and I exited the room to get ready.

In short order we were walking out into the hall to head over to Akers' crime scene. It was almost three and it was so quiet in the building you could hear a pin drop if it weren't for the sound of our walking along the hardwood tongue-in-groove thin slat flooring. Pushing the button to call the elevator started sounds that indicated the car was in the lobby and had to travel up to get us. We were soon traveling along the Manhattan streets and crossing Central Park.

"55 Central Park West. Looks like we're here. I just hope this isn't over the top and tips our hand", I said.

"I'm sure it won't. Not now anyway", Sarah replied. "And it looks like half the department is here. There's nowhere to park."

"Looked like this last time. Nothing unusual", I said as I stopped the car in the street. "Sarah, take over while I step over there and call Akers again. If you find a place to park I'll wait here for you and we'll go up together."

"Alright."

We stepped out of the car and Sarah got in under the wheel as I walked to the corner phone booth. I pulled the door closed mainly so the light would let me see to dial the number. After a few rings I heard a simple, "Hello."

"Hi. This is Frank DeGrae. I need to speak to Akers."

"Yes sir. Hold on just a minute. I'll get him." I could see Sarah walking up the sidewalk when I heard, "Frank."

"Yeah Calvin. Is she there?"

"She is indeed my friend. But you need to get up here. She's wanting to go."

"I'm downstairs on my way up now. Bye", I said as I set the receiver back on the cradle and pulled the door open. Stepping out I said to Sarah, "She's up there now but Akers said we need to get up there." Sarah said nothing back and we picked up the pace.

Walking into the lobby I looked around for our escort and it didn't take long to find her. "Officer Brant", I called out. She turned around and I followed with, "Good morning. It's nice to see you again although I wish it were back at the DA's office rather than here again."

"Hello Mr. DeGrae. Lieutenant Akers is upstairs expecting you. They're in apartment 714. Will you be needing an escort to the apartment today?" she replied very business-like.

"Oh, I don't think that will be necessary but thank you for asking. We can find it", I answered as Sarah and I started for the elevators.

With Brant well behind us I said to Sarah, "That seems a little odd", and we stepped onto the center car already at the lobby with the door open. We moved to the back and turned around facing the door.

The operator pulled the gate as the door closed while asking, "Seventh floor?" With the activity already in the building and the time of day he already knew where we were going.

"Yes, please. Thank you", I answered.

Just as I spoke the elevator shuttered a bit and we began the climb. Sarah and I stood silent during the ride not wanting to discuss anything within earshot of anyone else. The climb to the seventh floor seemed slower than usual but I surmised it was just me wanting to get off. After what seemed like forever the car started to slow its ascent until finally easing to a standstill. The elevator operator announced we had arrived and pulled the gate and opened the door.

Stepping into the hallway and starting toward the right Sarah asked, "So that was Brant?"

"It was. I still haven't figured out how she manages to wind up on all of these. I did find out there is a special unit the PD formed to use female officers on major crime scenes. It's to handle miscellaneous duties to free up detectives and male officers if something violent comes up. But I checked back and she's been out on all of these. Coincidence?"

"Probably not, but it could be. Let's let this thing play out", Sarah said.

"You're right."

Once again it was a breeze to find the apartment. The hall was choked with detectives and uniforms. We met Akers in the hallway this time. No one was inside yet. As I approached Akers with Sarah in tow he looked at me and nodded. We followed him inside.

Emerging from the modest hallway into the vastness of the Edwardian styled parlor I asked Akers, "So where is Marion and her sidekick?"

"On their way. I spoke to her just before I called you. She said she would call Waters and come up with a reason she needed to come with her."

"Good", I said.

Officer Watson entered the room. "Excuse me." We turned to look in his direction and he continued. "Lieutenant Akers?"

"Yes."

"Mr. O'Dwyer and Special Agent James Ellison are here to see you sir."

"Thanks. Send 'em on back here."

"Yes sir", he said turning back to the hall.

"So Frank, can you let me in on what you've got cooked up? Looks like you've got the Who's Who of New York City coming to this party. I wouldn't be surprised if the Mayor himself didn't show up."

"The day is young Calvin. Don't count anything out just yet."

Before our conversation could move along any further our two guests of honor entered the parlor. Before we could exchange proper salutations Miss Marion McKinley and her assistant Bonnie Waters filed in right behind them. Marion glanced around the room and when she spotted her boss standing nearby she appeared to have seen a ghost.

"Good morning Marion", I said. "How've ya' been?"

Looking back at me with the same lost lamb look she replied, "Uh, fine Frank. I've been alright. Same as usual. And you?" in a most uncharacteristic manner. Everyone could tell the sight of O'Dwyer was most disconcerting to her but she dared not question anyone about it. That in itself was strange that she did not.

"Miss Waters", Lieutenant Akers said as he touched the brim of his hat and slightly bowed his head. She nodded in response without speaking yet displayed a slight smile.

As we continued with our social exchanges and conversations a few more guests began to arrive. Mr. Carnaggio from the crime lab arrived with Tommy Milano from 'the Pit'. Not long after, our Officer Brant arrived, having been summoned from the lobby. Mr. Valentine arrived immediately afterward. Even Lieutenant Akers was surprised at that. The stage was just about set to start the show.

"Well it looks like just about everyone is here so I guess we'll start now with why we're all here", I said. "As you all know the nature of the call we're here on this morning is the homicide of a Mr. Andrew Holland of this address. It has been reported to all to be a repeat of the previous five murders over the last several months. The five victims having been dubbed members of the 'Dead Club' by those of us in the trenches working on this every day. The key being they have all been killed in exactly the same unusual way. It has also been learned they all have one additional thing in common with one another and that is why we are here today. We definitely have a serial killer among us and that person is in this room with us now."

In a more traditional tone Marion McKinley chimed in with, "If this is another of your 'Dead Club' murders why are we all standing out here chatting away doing nothing? Where is this victim? Is the crime scene in this apartment?"

"Relax Marion. The crime scene is right here in this room. There is no murder and Mr. Holland is still alive and well. We used his name to stage an event we knew everyone would come out to."

"No murder! Have you lost your mind getting all of us out here and there's no murder?" she replied.

"It took some doing but we finally figured Andrew Holland was the most likely candidate to be our killer's next victim. You see, he was acquitted of the death of a girlfriend not long ago. No one here knows what really happened in that case so we just have to rely on our court system to sort it out. All of us but you Marion. You and Miss Waters there know a great deal about it. Your names are all over the files associated with the prosecution of Mr. Holland."

"I don't understand. What on Earth are you talking about? Are you suggesting I know anything about these murders other than my prosecuting the victims for crimes before they died?"

"Did I say that?"

"I don't know what you're saying", Marion continued.

"Well hold onto your hat. You're about to find out", Sarah interjected.

"Thank you Sarah", I said. "You see everyone, Sarah just got back from a visit to Philadelphia and she learned quite a bit there. It seems our very own Officer Brant here hails from that part of the world and had a pretty rough time growing up in Pennsylvania."

"What? You investigated me? What would make you think I had anything to do with this?" asked Brant.

"Did you kill these men?" I asked.

"I haven't killed anyone Mr. DeGrae and I find this line of questioning most insulting", she replied.

"Can you explain why you're accusing one of my officers, Mr. DeGrae?" asked Mr. Valentine.

"Yes, Frank. Please expound", said Mr. O'Dwyer.

"Thank you gentlemen. I would be glad to. Sarah found out that Officer Brant's father worked for the Delaware and Hudson Coal Company back in the 20s when she was a child. In fact, it was in the summer of 1921 when her father was killed in a mine explosion at Wilkes Barre in their Tunnel #2."

"Mr. DeGrae! Please", pleaded Brant.

"Almost a hundred men perished in this accident. Needless to say the impact on the surviving families was horrific. Cynthia's mother even moved to Philadelphia thinking she could build a better life there for them. The intent was good but it wasn't to be."

"Cynthia Brant's mother soon met a man she thought would be the answer to their wants and needs", Sarah continued. "The romance blossomed and she moved this man into their home."

"Miss Landers, do we have to air this out in front of everyone?" Brant asked in a pleading tone.

"Is there anything you would like to add or tell us?" I asked.

"No. No there isn't Mr. DeGrae. It's just this stuff is very personal. And very painful. I just wish it would go away. Please stop torturing me."

"Mr. DeGrae", said Valentine.

"Give me just a minute. I assure you we are going somewhere with this."

"Alright, Mr. DeGrae. One minute", answered Valentine.

"Alright Sarah. You were over there. Please continue", I said.

"Thanks Frank. Anyway, there was an incident that would change things for Cynthia and her mother forever. An incident involving this boyfriend of her mother. There had been a series of fights and beatings Cynthia's mother was involved in with this man and Cynthia, as a child, witnessed them all. One particular day Cynthia came home to see the boyfriend on top of her mother up in the middle of the bed. While holding her mother down and choking the life out of her. Both of his powerful working class hands were wrapped around her throat crushing the air from her body. Cynthia yelled at him to stop but he was oblivious to her presence. Cynthia then did the only thing she thought she could. She had to stop the attack and save her mother's life."

"Oh god!" Brant cried out. "Please stop!"

I picked up where Sarah stopped. "Cynthia ran to the next room and picked up the first thing she saw she thought she could use as a weapon. A weapon to save her mother from certain death. She picked up a large pair of shears from her mother's sewing table. A very large pair with 10-inch blades and large black handles. She ran back into her mother's bedroom, jumped onto the bed over the footboard, and onto his back. She then sank the blades of these scissors to the handle in the middle of his back. He died almost instantly, collapsing directly down onto her mother with Cynthia on top of him."

"I did not kill that man. My mother killed him during that fight. And she was cleared of any wrong doing."

"That's what your mother told authorities. She took responsibility to protect you but we now know different. What you did to defend your mother was justified. It's okay. It may even be the reason you chose to become a cop. But recently things have gotten out of hand. You've assumed the role of protector of weak women abused and killed by men."

"And what's wrong with that Frank? Aren't all cops crusaders? Defenders of the oppressed and weak?" asked Marion.

"To an extent I suppose you're right. But when it turns into vigilantism and murder the judicial crusader becomes a criminal."

"Frank, Officer Brant is no killer or criminal. She is a good cop and you're really stepping out of line accusing her", replied Marion.

"Mr. DeGrae, I think we've heard enough of this", followed Valentine.

"Mr. Valentine. Miss McKinley. I have never accused Officer Brant of anything improper or illegal. Your own imaginations and assumptions have done that. What I was going to say, if I may be allowed to continue, is Officer Brant has of late, become close friends with our Assistant District Attorney Marion McKinley. She pays her a visit at her officer almost daily and has been assigned to a joint bureau created by the NYPD and Prosecutor's Office to focus on Domestic Assaults in the city at McKinley's request."

"And what is the problem Frank?" asked McKinley.

"There is no problem with that but it shows the foundation of what follows. You, Marion, have become disillusioned at the system you represent. You have listened to Brant's stories at length and then all the other victim's coming through your office to the point you've thought there must be a better way. The system is broken so you've taken it upon yourself to mete out justice."

"You're crazy."

"No Marion, you had Brant sent out to every one of these calls to offer a sense of support for you. And you have conveniently been the on-call ADA, and responded to the scene, of every one of the 'Dead Club' murders. Why? Coincidence? I checked the on-call schedule for your office. You were always scheduled for the mid-month weekend. Not to mention you were always out on a date when you were called out. Always showing up at the crime scene dressed to kill. Oh, I made a joke there. Sorry."

"Really? That's all you have. You better do better than that Frank or your days of being a detective have just come to an end", she said.

"The dates you had been out on were the dead men you showed up for as the on-call ADA. Like the arsonist who sets the fire then stays to watch the fire trucks. You lured them to their death and returned when the investigators showed up to steer their findings. Very clever."

"I have done no such thing."

"For another thing Marion, not a single interview or arrest has been made regarding any of these murders. Not one. Why are you dragging your feet on all these murders? And something happened at the McAghon crime scene, just upstairs from where we stand, that has bothered me since that day."

"Oh? Do tell."

"When I got there I took notice, and notes, of the scene. Details of the interior of his apartment. There was a small lady's clutch purse sitting on the end table in the parlor. You arrived sometime after me and walked directly back to the bedroom with Lieutenant Akers to see the body after a few choice words for me. When you came back up front and started on your way you scooped up the little clutch purse from the end table as if it were yours. It was yours but you had not set it down when you arrived. You left it behind after you killed him. You realized it after leaving and when you went back to cover your tracks you slipped that in. Very smooth."

"That's crazy. You can't prove anything."

"You didn't know where it was so you used Akers to walk throughout the entire apartment until you spied it on the table. You were very cool and collected with your mission and no one was the wiser as to what you had actually done."

"You're still reaching Frank."

"Tommy", I called out.

"Yeah Frank", Milano answered.

"Tell us about the murder weapons. All of them please."

"Alright Frank. Well, when the bodies were transported down to 'the Pit' they all still had the murder weapon in them. Scissors in the back. We naturally removed them during the autopsies and catalogued them."

"Interesting", said O'Dwyer.

"Yes sir. It is. Go ahead Tommy", I said.

"It turned out all these scissors were identical."

"Identical? Could you elaborate?" I asked.

"I can", he said. "In each case we removed a pair of J. Wiss & Sons Pinking Shears. These are the 10.5 inch model 'A' shears. They make a model 'B' pair that are 9 inches long but all these were the longer version."

"Carni, what else can you and your lab guys tell us about the scissors in question?" I asked.

"Well Frank, all of these came from the same lot and manufactured about the same time."

"Is this significant?" I asked.

"Where are we going with all this? Everyone here is busy. We don't have time for this Frank", Marion barked.

"Go ahead Carni", I said.

"Yeah, Frank. It is. It would seem to indicate they left the factory together as part of a case shipment."

"Thanks buddy." I turned back to face Marion and continued. "We managed to secure a search warrant on your apartment based on an affidavit signed by me. It would seem my earlier statement was at least good enough to supply probable cause."

"You've really gone too far this time Frank DeGrae", McKinley growled.

"No Marion. We found the case of shears you purchased and the remaining scissors still in the box." Marion's facial contortions quickly transformed. She suddenly had the appearance of a lost child. "The number missing is the same as those recovered from the bodies."

"Uh..."

"And the lab checked and confirmed all pairs were of the same lot number and the murder weapons shipped in that box. We also found the craft shop you purchased them from. They remember the sale because it's a retail store that never sells full cases of these things to a single customer."

"Frank-", said Marion with a completely resigned expression.

"And finally Marion, your last victim didn't even have the benefit of an acquittal. The others had been tried and acquitted but McAghon had only been arraigned and released on bond. You had elevated yourself to pass judgement even before the court did. Not to mention in each and every case not a single fingerprint; not even a smudge, was found. It gave the impression these were not murders of passion but rather pre-meditated and well planned. And finally, you chose this method from the stories your new friend Brant told you of her childhood horror. In the event this game unraveled you could build a circumstantial case around her."

Marion's countenance had completely transformed into a beaten and vulnerable victim begging for mercy. On the verge of tears and with quivering lips she managed to eke out, "But Frank. You don't understand. These were evil men. I knew they were murderers and would kill innocent victims again."

"You bitch!" screamed Brant.

Mr. O'Dwyer turned to Marion and said, "Miss McKinley, you're fired."

"What?" she replied through tears.

"And you're under arrest. Mr. Valentine?"

"Yes sir?" Valentine answered.

"Would you please remove Miss McKinley from the scene?"

"I would be happy to."

"No! Wait!" Marion cried out as two uniformed officers entered the room and they escorted the three from the room.

"Wow. I would have never guessed that", said Brant. "I guess that wraps that up then", and started toward the door.

"Just a moment Officer Brant", Sarah said. Brant stopped abruptly and turned to Sarah but said nothing.

"There is a little matter of an incident involving a Mr. Jonathan Stephens."

"Who is that?"

"Incredible. You drove all the way up to New Rochelle to kill a guy for McKinley and you say you don't know who it is?"

"I beg your pardon", Brant said.

"Officer Brant", I said. "I think you know what Miss Landers is talking about. Do you recall a night not too long ago where you drove Miss McKinley's BMW 328 to the Glen Island Casino? Where you met Mr. Stephens before following him to the Glenwood Inn a few hours later?"

"I don't recall any of that."

"That car she had you drive wasn't her's. She borrowed it from the victim, Mr. Stephens."

"She told me it was hers. She said... wait..." Brant said in a hurried, almost reflexive manner before catching herself.

"You and Miss McKinley have become very close during the past few months. That in itself is not a problem but the two of you have started a confederation to administer justice to the evil sexual harassing men of the world."

"Look, I can help you secure a conviction against her. I didn't do anything but she did tell me some things and tried to draw me in. I wouldn't go along with her plans to kill so I was being blackmailed for what I had done for her", Brant confessed.

"Look Cynthia, we put in a lot of hours retracing your steps in New Rochelle. You should know how this works. We know it was you and have a list of witnesses up there that will tell what they saw in court. Under oath. You killed him for her over some petty harassing thing between them years ago. What was in it for you?"

"I want a lawyer."

"Lieutenant Akers, I present to you the killer of Mr. Jonathan Stephens, Esquire", I said to Calvin as he drew his service revolver.

"Don't move Miss Brant. I'll take your weapon", Akers said to her. Other officers behind her also moved in and took hold of her arms. They placed handcuffs on her and led her away with no further conversation.

"Well Calvin it looks like we're pretty much done here. How about breakfast at Horn and Hardy's again. I'm buying."

"Just a minute Mr. DeGrae. We still have a small matter to address here before we move along", said Ellison.

"Oh, that's right. My apologies sir", I answered and then pointed toward Miss Waters. "She's all yours. We have nothing on her so the Feds are welcome to her."

"Now what is this about?" asked Waters.

Lieutenant Akers said, "I'll have a couple of my guys help you get her to your office."

"Thanks Akers. You guys are great."

Two more officers took Waters into custody and despite her protests was escorted from the apartment.

23

Sarah walked into the room with four cups of coffee secured in a sectioned off cardboard carrier. I followed with a box of donuts and sack of goodies for the coffee. Since both of my hands were full she stopped to let me pass and then pulled the door closed. The receptionist stopped typing and looked up at the spectacle entering her domain.

"Oh, good morning Mr. DeGrae. Miss Landers", she said.

"Lieutenant Akers just got here about ten minutes ago. I'll see if he's busy."

Sarah set the coffee down on the front edge of the desk, removed one of the cups and offered it to Mrs. Morrison still seated. "Here. We picked one up for you too", Sarah said. "He's expecting us. One of these is his."

With a smile came, "Why thank you. That's so thoughtful. Please go on in. I'm sure he won't mind."

I said, "Thank you Mrs. Morrison" and Sarah turned the knob to Calvin's office. Calvin was already on the phone to someone but managed to still hear us come in. He looked up but never missed a beat with his telephone conversation. Sarah and I went ahead and set everything down on a nearby work table. As Calvin raised a hand and nodded in our direction we continued setting the table for our world class continental breakfast.

Still at work setting the breakfast table we heard the phone click as Calvin hung the receiver back on its cradle and, "Well good morning boys and girls. What do we have here?"

Looking around I could see him walking from behind the desk and Sarah answered, "Coffee and donuts Lieutenant. Hungry?"

"We made a run by Mayflower's. Hope you like crullers", I added.

"I could probably force myself to have one if I must", he said as he picked up a napkin.

"Any news?" I asked.

"As a matter of fact, yes. You two will be glad to know your little vacation cruise to Florida turned out to be most valuable to Mr. Hoover."

"I'm all ears."

"It seems our mild mannered Miss Bonnie Waters, aka Sibone Walters, is a pivotal member of a spy network headquartered here in New York."

"No kidding."

"No. That was Ellison on the phone. He told me they're going to use her as a double agent to work on pulling down the whole network. This is of the greatest secrecy so not a word. In fact, I'm only telling you guys because they're putting her back on the street and in her old job. You'll be seeing her around again so just steer clear of her when you do."

"Right."

"What we do know so far is the Nazis have placed spies throughout New York in various key occupations. This is to facilitate logistics and information gathering for Germany in preparation for future hostilities between our countries. Waters came up on our radar when McAghon was killed because he was also a part of this spy ring."

"So that explains why McAghon was an exchange clerk but lived in that apartment. I wondered how he could afford to live at 55 Central Park West on that pay."

"And it explains why there was a mystery woman checking up on him at the morgue. A mystery woman we now know is Waters. She got a little sloppy with how she handled her visits and pretty much tipped her hand then. And when you two followed her aboard the cruise ship we learned it was to pass information on to Germany with no possibility of being intercepted."

"We couldn't get word to you while we were still at sea without the radio shack operator knowing what we were doing. How did that get figured out so fast?" I asked.

"You're not the only genius Frank. Remember, I was standing across the street when you followed Waters into the terminal. It didn't take long to figure out what happened. FBI and Coast Guard intercepts along the coast revealed the cruise liner was collecting intelligence at the same time Waters was doing her thing. The Nazi government has been very smooth in their spy efforts but our guys have kept one step ahead. We still maintain diplomatic relations with Germany and they still have an ambassador here in New York but we're actually learning more about them than they'll ever know about us. And when the Feds are ready they'll throw out the net and pull the whole gang in at one time."

"I'm glad to know our little outing wasn't a waste of time after all", Sarah added.

"Oh no. quite the opposite. But your contribution to defending the country will never be known. All of this is classified at the highest levels. You can never mention any of this again."

"We understand Calvin. We're not in the spy business anyway. What's up with Marion and Brant?" I asked.

"It seems Brant got sucked into a pact with McKinley. They had become bosom buddies and Brant thought she and her career would blossom having an attorney and ADA as a friend."

"Poor stupid girl", said Sarah.

"May be, but she's now up for murder because of it and 'I'm sorry' won't get it. It seems to be shaping up that she was aware of McKinley's murders and helped to cover them up. Also making her an accomplice to those killings. Now Marion McKinley is a shark of a completely different color. I think her heart and motivations in the beginning were honorable and in the right place. After all, she did become a prosecuting attorney to put bad guys away. But somewhere along the way there was a misfire. A short circuit in her morality made it okay for her to kill acquitted killers. We may never know when, how, or why but I think we've seen the end of that problem too."

"Thanks for the update on all this Calvin. I guess we'll head back to finish up the last of our report narratives and, of course, submit our invoices."

"Look, do me a favor and send those bills straight on down to City Hall. It'll save me a headache and you'll get paid faster. A win-win for everybody", said Akers.

"Anything else?" I asked.

"Yeah. Get out of my office. I need a break."

"You need a break?"

"And leave the donuts."

THE END